Suicide By Ghost

a novella by Rose Sinclair

Creative Aces Publishing www.creativeacespublishing.com

Content Warning:

There's no suicide in this book, if you need help please reach out to National Suicide Prevention Lifeline or The Trevor Project.

Everyone can help protect LGBTQIA+ youth against homelessness by supporting True Colors United.

To all those funny queer people on the internet
who come in my time of plot bunny need like
a sign from God.

CHAPTER ONE

The ceiling featured twenty-six bullet holes left by long dead outlaws. If this had been a made for TV moment, a production crew would have added unnerving music. Maybe even a voice over that would make the audience believe that crime collects the most paranormal energy.

Reality had no such special effects. Just a man named Ryan, who felt nothing as he looked up. A lot of crime is about the heat of selfishness, or needing to survive an upcoming moment. None of that really mattered to Ryan. What brought him to the St. James Hotel was its name.

The stairs creaked under aging boots as Ryan walked up from the dining room. The hallway decor brought everything back to the past. The only tell that time marched on was a photo on the wall showing the buildings original name: Lambert's Inn.

Faith was what made this place haunted. Any sort of belief provided the needed staying power. Believing it was already haunted, changing the name to something with a 'deeper' meaning, all would do. Hauntings didn't even need consistent faith, even though seminary taught otherwise.

A creak vibrated towards Ryan as he took slow steps forward. The camera in his hand pointed toward the motion as it settled. The monitor displaced a tiny version of the world filtered through the night vision setting. It was dark, and when movement caught Ryan's eyes again, he was surprised he saw even that much. Above his head, a chandelier swayed from side by side in perfect silence.

"Do not be afraid."

For a moment he felt as if something heard, *understood*. But anything else was smothered by the memory of being schooled not to talk directly to spirits in the first place. Sharing his name was probably even more inadvisable, but he added it aloud anyways.

"My name is Ryan; do you have anything you need to say?"

Investigations have their own set of rules. Ghost hunting was all about being somewhere and waiting for any possibility. Exorcisms, on the other hand, were strict no nonsense events. Get in, get the demons out. The owner made it very clear he wanted the first. The removal of possible demons would tank this tiny town's economy. As much as it went against the church, at least people in town could eat with one allegedly on the loose. Having a Vatican certified exorcist visit only would add to the tourist value. Ryan wasn't completely sure how he felt about that, but did enjoy not having to worry about food.

A new chorus of creaks sounded off as Ryan visited another room. On a table, a vintage poker chip spinner drew his hand closer before he even consciously realized it. Hesitation be damned, he spun it around and spotted something tucked where cards were stored. His fingers dug out a rosary.

He tilted his hand and gravity pulled the rosary away. With a sigh, Ryan pulled off his bag, setting it on the table. He sorted past other equipment until he pulled out a magnetometer. It didn't look like much, but the small rectangular box could measure magnetic fields. He set up a camera next. The meter spiked as he surveyed the room around him, but he didn't notice.

When he swapped the devices, the meter leveled out. In the camera screen, Ryan looked calm, focused, professional, despite hoping that something would happen to him. Be dragged out of frame, have a shadowy figure appear over his shoulder. Something that would make people believe. Maybe even make him believe again too...

He collected nothing, besides more data. The exchange with the owner next morning wasn't any more inspiring. The man seemed more excited than reassured.

A stray cat joined them, staring at the two men as they spoke outside on the porch. After a moment, Ryan looked back, spinning a ring of keys around his fingers. He opened his mouth just as the cat did the same, but no meow followed. The cat stared a second longer before trotting off.

"Remember, don't talk directly to the spirits," Ryan said. "You'll only encourage them to be more physical."

The owner laughed, half-heartedly agreed, and gave thanks once again.

Ryan nodded and stepped down to his truck. It was red with a small cab and a mismatched camper shell over the back. He gently tossed, if that duality could equally exist at once, the ghost hunting equipment into the back before waving goodbye. This job was enough to take care of the truck, his food, and get him to the next stop.

Ryan pulled into a Catholic church two cities away, without needing to double check the address. He sat there, leaning against the steering wheel and wishing that feelings, like the gear, could be easily tossed somewhere when they weren't needed. Libraries and parks never held the same type of energy as a parish. Almost as if the land really was holy. *Or haunted,* like he thought on the more cynical days.

The parking lot was nearly full, and his truck's color stood out even in the very back. People moved freely to and from an annex building nearby, a clear sign that something besides mass was going on.

Ryan got out, checking his collar out of habit even though that style hadn't been around his neck for a while now. He and the church weren't exactly on speaking terms. Worse than the lack of consistent salary was the feeling of not quite being a part of the church, even as he looked around for the priest who had called him here.

The people gathered looked far more ready for a potluck than a bible study. Food was lined up along a short wall by the door, and volunteers greeted attendees and dished out brunch. After being a unified line, people broke out into their own groups, with rare mixing besides the occasional priest, deacon, or overly involved choir lead. It was oddly *white* after the historically dusty buildings.

Along another wall, there was a kid's group project, handprints and crosses cut out with krazy scissors. Next to it was Ryan's former classmate. College wasn't always enough to forge concrete friendships, but share a family secret with someone and they can get you halfway across the country.

"Boys will be boys," the woman next to the priest said. Her voice was sharp, and too sure of itself. There was cruelty in those words she didn't understand. But Ryan did, and it stopped him cold.

"We are all children of God here." The familiarity of the priest's voice got Ryan moving again. "And I must insist that your son is more respectful in the future, or I won't be able to invite him back for the lock in."

The woman started to object, but when Ryan walked up, she paused. "Okay, I'll talk to him about it. Thank you, Father Michael," she said, giving a forced smile to Ryan before excusing herself.

A cautious, quiet moment deliberately ticked on by until

no one was in earshot.

"Please tell me that isn't the family you want me to speak with, James."

"It's not," the priest with two first names said. Ryan raised his brow with something akin to doubt before Father Michael continued. "But you aren't going to like this family any more."

Ryan sighed, looking around the room in a trained way. "Why me? All you would say before is that you were looking for an exorcist. I'm sure I don't need to remind you that I'm not a part of the church anymore."

For a moment, Father James Michael held his gaze in a way where he looked nothing like a priest. Just a man, who seemed worried. "Because you are you."

That haunting statement made parting from the socializing parishioners even more jarring. They walked into a hushed church that was cold from the lack of people inside. The smell of unscented candles filled the air, and a small glow ran along the back. Two people were bent at the knee in prayer in the first pew. Ryan dipped his finger in a bowl of holy water, making the sign of the cross as he passed the door.

Father Michael stepped into the same pew as the couple. He placed a hand on the man's shoulder as his wife continued to near feverishly pray, either encouraged by the priest's presence or utterly unaware of it. Ryan stood back, his gut tighter from simply seeing these two than it had been with the stray comment before. Something wasn't right here. He could feel it.

When Ryan had been a child, he used to think that the air rushing out of a church was evil spirits leaving a hallowed place. That nothing impure could exist inside the doors without being overcome with the urge to flee. The air shifted as James made introductions, and Ryan knew once again that theory had been without merit. Something dark followed this couple.

"Your prayers have been heard," Father Michael said. He gestured over to Ryan. "This is Father Macy, the exorcist I mentioned. This is Mike and Karen Althaus. They think their son is possessed."

"Oh?" The words left Ryan's lips without much force, but they still echoed around the church before stations of the cross etched in glass and wood hushed them. This much, he had known. This much, and not much else.

If you did an internet search for 'signs your child is possessed,' the results would yield things like, 'Did your sweet child suddenly change into someone disrespectful? Or even violent?' Those who deeply believed in the paranormal often added strange happenings like eyes rolling back in their head. For too long, theories that childhood behavior was caused by demons or other creatures from fairy tales had been a result of ableism. So much so, they now taught certified exorcists on how to figure out whether mental health was a problem before assuming a spirit corrupted or controlled the person in question.

This couple's story had some of the signs that could cause some to consider investigating the unearthly: a new interest in the spiritual that was separate and secret from the rest of the family, a Ouija board found under a pile of laundry downstairs. The father claimed both things were clear evidence that their son had summoned evil.

"Could you help our family, Father?"

Hearing the title a second time felt no less strange. He had willfully walked away from it, and here it was once again. Ryan cleared his throat and worked on nodding before glancing over. "God willing."

The woman smiled brightly, as if that answer had been even better than a direct yes.

"You two should head home," Father Michael suggested. "Give me a call when your son comes back and we'll stop by."

They left like the last women had - appearing respectful in action, yet utterly oblivious to the true evil they were messing with.

Once it was empty, Ryan sat in the pew. He looked towards the hanging figure of Christ on the cross. In pain, yet celebrated. This pose was most common, but always his least favorite. More churches should have the Christ resurrected, the celebratory, transformative, life everlasting version of the man the religion was named after. This version always left him with the question: Did this count as torture porn or inspiration porn?

"Do you think their son is possessed?"

Michael pressed his lips together as if Jesus was being asked, but when no other voice spoke, he did. "I don't have the schooling to make that call."

"That wasn't my question."

James straightened the papers tucked into the pew, giving the hymns and envelopes attention. "No, but they refused all my attempts at help." Organized, but clearly not any more pleased, he stopped fussing. "That's why I called you. You are the only person I could think of that might be able to help."

CHAPTER TWO

The Althaus family lived in a farmhouse so old, it might have been in their name for generations. The windows were trimmed with handcrafted lace that had a daisy pattern. Darkness was not this place's problem.

A collection of crosses were proudly displayed on the wall. A bible sat on the table with bookmarks marking several passages. They'd been instructed to call after their son had returned, but upon being greeted they mentioned that he'd be back soon. Everyone sat in the living room as a slow cooker radiated the scent of a dinner also on hold.

The son walked in as if he knew what was inside. There was no half a second of surprise as he opened the door. One glance, and he headed upstairs.

"Andrew, come sit down," Karen said.

Andrew tilted his head sharply to the side, wondering if he could ignore her, before taking a step back towards everyone. He seemed to have zero intention of talking and instead stared blankly at the middle of the coffee table.

His parents were about to say something when Ryan cut them off. "What's on your hand?"

Andrew pulled his hand back so the black marks would be covered by the fabric of his long-sleeved shirt. He mumbled what sounded like a garbled 'nothing' as he looked at Ryan. There was a curious intelligence there that didn't seem more than human. Definitely lined with something - confusion or even maybe fear. Ryan, in slacks and a faded button up that had far too many tiny wrinkles, looked like an off-duty priest at best. His days of wearing a fresh pressed outfit everyday were gone.

"Who even are you?" the kid asked.

Father Michael filled him in, making it sound like no less than an intervention that had been suddenly sprung on him. Andrew's expression grew darker with each word, less of a brooding anger and more of a quiet, annoyed storm. Ryan pulled out his driver's license and slid it over to Andrew as the parents were now the ones growing lost. "May I speak to him alone?"

"I, well, shouldn't we…?" Karen glanced from one person to another, looking for reassurance.

Father Michael got up and waved a hand to the backyard. "Why don't you show me how your garden is going? It's been a while since I've seen the progress."

Andrew waited until all three of them were outside before reaching out and picking up the strange offering of an ID. When he did, Ryan could once again see the black marks written on his skin. It was a word, upside down from his angle. "What is that? Mal–maelstrom?'

"Maybe, so?"

"Do your parents think it is some secret devil worship thing?"

Andrew snorted. "Probably." He leaned back, seeming to enjoy the theory.

"Whirlpool, right?"

"What?"

Andrew pulled back further when he thought Ryan was going to touch him, but he appeared to regret it when Ryan just took his ID back. He suspected it hadn't told him anything interesting, anyway. Under Andrew's watchful eye, he pulled out his cellphone and typed on it for a few seconds.

"'Maelstrom. A powerful whirlpool, or a situation or state of confused movement or violent turmoil. Turbulence, chaos, upheaval.'" When Ryan's eyes met the kid sitting across from him again, he smiled. "It's a good word."

Andrew didn't seem to believe he wasn't being mocked, or pandered to in that, 'Trust me, man, I'm a cool youth pastor' way. He stared for a moment, eyes looking over Ryan again as if he didn't fit in the picture he saw. "You're not like the other people they brought," he said.

Ryan looked over his shoulder towards the garden with an amused exhale not quite muffled by his movement. "You aren't wrong. Do you want to tell me about what's happening?"

Now the hallmarks of teenage rebellion started to show. Eye rolls, slouching. But nothing hinted at the demonic. Maybe he was just goth-leaning with a reckless attitude toward his body that might cause him to someday agree to a stick and poke tattoo from a friend, or even give himself one if he was bored enough.

Ryan carried on, even if the silent treatment was in the forecast. "Your parents said they found a hidden Ouija board. Were you and some other boy messing around?"

The pulse in Andrew's neck jumped at the last question. There was indeed something about this boy.

"Can I ask you a kind of weird question?"

"All of you is weird."

Ryan ignored that, the snap of someone who felt cornered. There were probably very few spaces in this house where Andrew could just be without eyes watching him. "What's your least favorite Bible verse?"

"Least?"

Ryan nodded. "I heard someone describe six different

verses as bullets in a gun. Said those six were used harm people while over two thousand other verses went ignored, largely the ones that were designed to help those in need. Those are my least favorite. I won't read the six to you, but one is from Leviticus. Do you know it?"

Andrew nodded and grew increasingly pale.

Ryan smiled, trying to put the teen at ease. "I should go talk to your parents."

Andrew was frozen until Ryan made it to the kitchen. He quickly stood up. "Wait!" It was loud enough they both paused, thinking people might come back inside. Andrew swallowed hard. It looked like the physical space between them was the only thing making him feel safe enough not to just run out of the house. "Do you think I'm possessed?"

Ryan's hand floundered for a moment. "There ain't a thing wrong with you, kid. And I intend to tell your parents that and only that."

The almost always silent Mike Althaus was nowhere in sight when Ryan stepped out. He could tell at a glance that a lot of money was poured into the landscaping here, and into a large looking shed that marked the edge of the property. Father Michael had a tired, distant look in his eyes that he used to get when some teacher droned on, like they were first year students who didn't understand anything. Karen didn't notice, as she rambled about the carrots she was growing. The chicken in the coop seemed to agree. Father Michael spotted Ryan and suddenly looked like he had just been given salvation, from this conversation at least. His bright eyes alerted Karen. She placed her hands together, praying for good news.

"I feel like I should say this in front of both you and your husband," Ryan said.

"I'll go get him!" At the pace of a brisk walk, she headed to the shed.

Ryan looked over at his friend, giving him a look that said too much to be read fully. "You were right."

Father Michael lifted a brow.

"I didn't like them."

The priest's shake of his head alarmed Andrew's father as he approached, jogging over with a frown on his face. "I knew it," he said. "That boy isn't right."

"There's nothing to fear," Ryan said. "Your son is safe and sound. I see no signs of a demon or any other spiritual attachments around him."

"Really?" The mother was bright, hopeful, beaming. The father looked doubtful, like he wouldn't believe anything this technically Vatican man might say until he started to hear what he wanted.

Ryan's mouth downturned. "There is something unholy around, however. Hate, that will infect everyone and everything here if you don't continue with Father Michael's guidance after I leave."

"Tell me," Karen said fervently. "Tell us what we need to do."

Ryan glanced to his friend, their trusted priest, who gave a quick nod to continue. "You don't love your son unconditionally. You allowed hate to enter your heart."

"Now look here," Mike said. His wife's sobs cut him off. He shot Ryan dirty look before he whispered condolences to his wife.

"I'm sorry this isn't the answer you wanted," Ryan said, turning away for half a second, "Take care of the gift you have been given. Each person is made in God's image; your son needn't reflect yours. All I have left to offer is that God doesn't grant anyone a blessing to exorcise someone's personal demons. You must do that yourself."

CHAPTER THREE

Ryan Robert Macy, former priest and freelancer exorcist, was from a family that had always been heavily involved with the not-so-holy Catholic Church. Named in honor of grandfathers who had served the church their whole lives. Several years ago, Ryan had a conscious uncoupling with the Church. It resulted in his faith, even his outright belief in God without The Holy See, being shaken down to the roots.

At the age of five, a mustard sized seed of faith sprouted. Ryan hadn't been able to move a mountain range, but he had done what many deemed impossible. Even though to him, it was always the way of things.

"Momma, momma, I'm a boy!" called Ryan. He ran into her office holding his birth certificate.

Confused, she held her hand out to take the paper from him. Printed there, along with everything else she already knew to be true, was a little black M.

"And, you're happy about this?"

She sounded concerned, but Ryan didn't waver in the slightest. "God knew," he said, smiling.

She smiled back. How she missed that in the first place was beyond her, but it felt like nothing short of a miracle if this was what made her son happy. She bent down to his level, gingerly offering the birth certificate back. "He must have. This paper is a gift from God, Ryan. Go put it back where you found it. We must be sure to take care of it."

Believing that this was a miracle, Ryan went to school with the hope of becoming a priest. The Church itself scrutinized his documents more than the school system ever had, and more than what was needed for his driver's license. Since the government agreed Ryan had always been a boy, so followed the church.

People said God works in mysterious ways, but what was even stranger was how a single blessed typo opened so many doors for Ryan. When he got older, he realized how unfair it was that he was given this blessing when other trans men were not. Some pointless, even cruel, hurdles had been cleared for him.

Only once did someone find out that Ryan wasn't cisgender without telling them first. It was during a medical emergency where EMTs were called, by none other than Ryan's roommate and fellow seminary student, James Michael. The two of them talked about it after Ryan's hernia surgery. And the only thing that changed between them was that Ryan was actually able to be a bit less cautious about his scars - old, new, and metaphoric.

But all true evil tries to return, and transphobia in the church still cut. As a distraction, Ryan quietly took the extra classes he needed to be an exorcist. Avoiding the living in favor for the demonic worked for a while, until the fact that the church wasn't looking like it would ever unconditionally love him back was too much to bear. Before he could no longer hold his tongue, Ryan left the church on as good of terms as possible when leaving everything you knew behind.

He got his red truck used, and put the first camper he found on it. It had faux wood siding, and was slightly taller than the truck itself for the extra head room. Windows on three sides opened out for air and the illusion of more space. It wasn't a true home, but it was a great for camping and traveling the paranormal circuit.

Most people preferred that he wasn't actually sent by the Vatican, since they hadn't been able to get the church's attention in the first place. Others simply didn't understand the strict rules the Catholic Church followed, and thought without real care either way that he was still an official part of it.

That path had been serving him well until today, where an informal college reunion brought him back to a church and to people who were less than accepting. But what does one do to protect a child that isn't theirs?

"Ryan. Ryan!"

Ryan blinked hard, seeing the room again for the first time. Church, community hall, people passing out donuts after mass. Right. "Sorry, Father Michael," he said, shaking his head. "I was thinking about something."

"No slacking off now that I actually hired you for something that pays." The joke had a cheerfulness that showed how Michael had won his position as the favorite here. It was a tease that said, 'I'm helping you, gosh darn it, and won't stop until you realize you are worth it.' If Ryan had to say God gave his friend anything in particular, it would be that uniquely balanced tone.

"Momma always said a college education would get me places." Ryan mirrored James as he picked up a box of stuff the church used and reused every year for a bible camp. "Maybe she should have been more specific."

James laughed. "Have you seen her recently?"

"Couple months ago."

They made a few more trips back and forth pulling boxes

out from one area to another only slightly closer. Sometimes the pastor did grunt work and sometimes he tried to save souls. Life was a mixed bag like that.

A little later in the afternoon, the two lent a hand counting the collections. Normally a deacon and his wife were in charge, but they were currently off on vacation. Everyone in the small room next to the church had volunteered, but a regular who made it clear they silently thought they should be in charge wasn't so thrilled with Ryan joining. Maybe he was giving off a vibe that said 'poor,' and therefore 'untrustworthy'. Or maybe the guy was just an ass that couldn't overrule Father Michael. Instead of being kicked out, Ryan was given the duty of dropping coins into an automatic sorter. This way the most he could possibly steal was a row of quarters worth a whole ten bucks.

If it was meant to be a punishment, he really didn't care. This was far easier than when he was a kid and the only help he had to sort the coins were plastic tubes that coins would slide out of once full.

Afterwards, James and Ryan caught an early dinner together before he had to be Father Michael again and head out to the hospital to give someone their last rites.

Ryan was thankful he got to miss out on that part. The first time he learned about death as a child was when his grandparents brought him along to give communion to those in the hospital who couldn't make it to mass. The blessings were a courtesy, but hospitals forever more were places of death in his mind.

Father Michael dropped him off at the curb near his car, where Ryan spotted a kid sitting alongside the annex building. He stood up. His backpack made him look like he just got out of school and was waiting for the bus. The streetlights beamed a halo down on him.

"I was starting to worry I missed you."

"Something wrong? What are you doing here?" The church was the last place Ryan thought he'd see Andrew willingly kill time at.

"I need a favor."

"Oh-kay?"

"Can I tag along with you for a while? Just until I get some things figured out."

"How old are you? Aren't you in school?"

"Yeah, that's one of the things I need to figure out. I could probably GED then take some community college online classes wherever I am. See?" Andrew grinned. "Thought that part out already."

Ryan glanced down at the curb, wondering if he should sit down and try to convince a minor to go back to his bigoted parents. Maybe God put the kid in his path. *Well,* a priest did at the very least. The only witness around was a statue of Saint George. It was tall enough to be a person if you counted the thick square stone base - a martyr, and patron saint of nothing. Least nothing he could remember. If God was leaving signs, they certainly ran out.

Ryan clicked his tongue, failing a way to find a soft way to ask what was on his mind. "Did you run away or get kicked out?"

"Does it matter?"

"To the police, it probably does."

"Fine." Andrew bit the word down. "You encouraged my parents to be more 'loving' and I thought, 'hey, maybe they mean it. So, I came out to them. Well, apparently it was more shocking than being a fucking demon, because my dad told me to get out. I don't think he meant for good, but I'm not going back. I thought... God, it's so stupid. I thought maybe you understood. You know that I'm... that I'm gay."

Now here came a truth Ryan was and wasn't ashamed of, something he thought might have been known before this request, and it had nothing to do with identity either. "You do know I sleep in the back of this truck, right?"

"Oh." Andrew pulled on the front of his backpack straps, chewing on his lip. "How bad can it be? Come on, please? If you get tired of me you can just drop me off in the next town or something. And if you say no, I'll just hitchhike with someone else."

"I'm a 35-year-old trans man," Ryan said. "I feel you already know I'm not going to let a gay teen try their luck on the street, if possible. Let's go."

"Fucking yes. Thank you." Andrew eagerly made his way towards the truck, pausing with his hand on the door. "You're not going to scold me if I don't say marshmallow swear words, are you?"

Ryan chuckled. "Haven't heard that one in a while, and no." The car was older, so even if Andrew hadn't stopped to ask, he would have been stuck until Ryan leaned over and flipped the manual lock.

Andrew pulled his backpack off, glancing back to the bed of the truck. There was a large cushion laid out between the wheel wells and carpet sticking out of the bottom. It would be tight with two, but doable. Instead of asking to throw his stuff back there, Andrew pulled it on his lap as he sat in the passenger seat. Ryan kept the truck nice, no tears or marks on the seats, and it didn't smell of anything, really. A glance back showed the dome light cover had yellowed over time. Besides that, it was as if the truck had been pulled out of the past brand new.

"Wow, this is old," Andrew said.

"Now, that sort of language you might need to watch."

"Does it have a name?"

"Ray."

"Why? Is that some sort of God is the Light thing?"

"Nah." Ryan put the truck in reverse and changed gears before gesturing to the keys. On the ring was a translucent plastic blue keychain. "When I got this truck, that was on it, and I didn't know if it was the original dealer's name or owner's. But I felt like the car was naming itself, so I went with it."

"I like it." Andrew smiled, a little forced, like he was out of practice in actively being sincere these days. "So... Is Father Michael going to be mad at you? I don't want to get you in trouble."

"I'm sure it will be fine, but it's probably better if he doesn't know the details."

Andrew nodded and the conversation died off for about twenty minutes. They weren't driving fast enough to blur the surroundings as they left town. Empty lots were just empty to Ryan, but to Andrew they had meaning. Short cuts to friend's houses, and tales about his first kiss with a boy, lost as they drove past in silence.

"So," Andrew finally said, "where are we going?"

"You said the next town over, so that seemed as good a place as any."

"I didn't mean that literally. You don't have anywhere to be?"

"Nope," Ryan said. "Already completed the tri-city area, so I normally head to next closest of any value."

"What about your job? I can't imagine the church has you go around briefly talking to homophobic church goers."

Ryan shrugged. "I ghost hunt."

"What? I thought you were a priest."

"I was. Now I ghost hunt."

Andrew laughed. Ryan had to glance over before he realized the kid actually enjoyed that answer more.

"Like Scooby-Doo."

"Ha. Yeah, but with less white men in costumes."

CHAPTER FOUR

They stopped at the first 24-hour diner they found. It wasn't extremely late, but around here, almost everything else closed by six. There had been a few local bars, but Ryan didn't drink, and Andrew couldn't. As they opened the door, the scent of pine cleaner was strong enough to hit them in the face.

Traveling had been a quiet affair, and even now as the two slid into a booth there were as few words as possible. Both seemed unsure of what they had gotten themselves into. Ryan consoled himself with the thought that his phone would send him an Amber Alert if Andrew's parents reported him missing. On the flip side, Andrew kept checking his own phone, seeming increasingly disappointed that no texts were coming in.

Andrew leaned his head against the window, angled so he had a view of the parking lot. Ryan hoped that truck of his did feel like a ray of hope, but he was in no way going to push the cheese factor right now.

The cutlery wrapped in a napkin had a hushed click as it was set down on the table by the busboy. "Your waitress will be right with you."

With a quick thanks, Ryan watched him go before returning his sole attention to Andrew. "You definitely should eat something. I checked the map, there won't be much after this."

"I can take care of myself."

The comment was a knee jerk more than anything else. Ryan sucked his teeth before giving up on trying to say anything of value and instead focused on the menu.

The pancakes looked good, but he had an overriding urge to get something shareable in case Andrew decided not to order at all. Ryan had never been a father, never even been in a serious relationship, and the only priests he knew with kids had joined late. They hadn't imparted much wisdom, but making sure your sad looking passenger had leftovers seemed like 101.

Andrew ordered a smoothie, which surprised Ryan. He didn't have the time to figure out if that counted as food or as a drink before he had to place his own order. "Chicken strip meal, please, with a coke."

A hacking smoker's cough almost shook the air as well as the lungs of a woman at the counter. Ryan fished around for the ketchup bottle in a caddy, but didn't find it behind the trio of syrup flavors. He got up and took the bottle from an empty table next to them, so he didn't have to bother anyone. "You ever play those crane games?" he asked as he sat down.

Andrew's brow pulled tight. He glanced over his shoulder to see a couple of machines he had missed by the door. "Yeah, I used to play all the time."

"I've never been good at them." Ryan half stood in his seat to pull out his wallet, then passed a twenty over. "Try your luck. I bet it beats just sitting here waiting for the order."

If Andrew was too cool for the game, he didn't show it. He scooped up the cash and headed over to play, studying the glass box of stuffed animals for a moment before even inserting the bill.

Ryan watched a bit, but after the first two tries he got bored and scrolled through his phone until the waitress arrived. She put the chicken strips down and Andrew returned with a stuffed Yoshi plush and change. He sat the medium sized green dinosaur on the table, adjusting the creature until he was sitting properly with his orange feet out in front of him.

"I wanted to get a power up mushroom, but their red tops were too big for the claw to really grab."

"That's fair. This guy's pretty soft and grabble. How many tries did it take you?"

"How about you mind your business," Andrew laughed before unwrapping a straw for the smoothie.

Ryan raised his brow up in surprise, but he was tickled by the reply more than anything else. The waitress came by after a while, asking if anything was needed, and Ryan asked for a box. His meal was deliberately only half eaten. When she returned with the box and the check, he ruined the ticket by adding dessert to the order. Andrew had been watching the rest of his smoothie slowly melt into juice before he glanced up.

"Can I head to the truck?"

"Yeah." Ryan fished out his keys to hand them over. "You can lie down in the back if you're tired."

Andrew was a couple steps towards the door before Ryan called for him to wait.

"Take the leftovers, please? You can have some if you get hungry. I gotta wait for the cheesecake to come and pay."

A tiny part of Ryan's gut expected Andrew to take his truck as well as the rest of his food. Then he wondered if the kid could even drive a stick. It wasn't a skill that was needed as much anymore. Ryan watched Andrew through the window, just to see. It took him a little bit of time to figure out which key went to the camper, but no grand theft auto.

Ryan left a nice tip and no cheesecake behind, and found

Andrew sleeping in the back of the truck. The blankets were still piled to the side, suggesting he hadn't meant to fall asleep. *Ah, quiet staring meant tired.*

"Magical monster?" Ryan asked with his phone to his ear. "That's what they are claiming?" If his tone hadn't been clear, that fact that he was pacing further displayed his doubt. Although, to be fair, that's just what Andrew assumed. He'd just woken up in the back of the truck. "It's probably just a wolf pack," Ryan continued, "No, I guess there's no reason not to look."

Andrew rubbed his eyes and ignored whatever that was. It was morning again, the sun just high enough that it gave everything a soft even brightness. The truck had moved, now outside a brick hotel. The first level was full of large glass planes with red awnings that made it look cafe-like.

When Ryan hung up, Andrew opened one of the side windows and leaned out on his arms. "Hey, so, where are we?"

"Las Vegas—"

"What the hell? How long was I asleep?"

"Las Vegas, New Mexico. About an hour from where we were."

"Oh. I always forget there's two." Definitely more than an hour had passed, so they must have stopped here for the night. "Did you even sleep?"

"In the cab." Ryan gestured towards the front. "I didn't want to risk waking you up. If you are feeling like it, I'm going to head inside. I can introduce you to the closest haunted location I could find."

Andrew crawled out of the back. "Is that what the call was about?"

"No, there's a park, about thirty minutes outside of the heart of Albuquerque. Might even be drunk teens, but it's another lead."

"Cool. Actually, it's fucking cold out here with this wind. Let's get inside." Seconds after stepping into the Plaza Hotel, Andrew nodded to himself. "Oh yeah. This is definitely still New Mexico." The Plaza was a historical building that wanted to keep that vibe, which meant wood floors, mostly wood chairs, and tables that were also likely wood hidden under white tablecloths. Anything that looked new looked worse.

"If you get bored, there is a Light Sanctuary in town. It projects rainbows across the floor and walls," Ryan said.

If anyone else said it, Andrew would have thought it was a joke at his expense. Instead he gave a non-committal grunt before checking for WiFi. "I'd rather see if there are any ghosts."

Andrew let Ryan go do whatever he normally did, which he assumed was asking strangers if they needed an exorcist, and fielding their 'are you fucking kidding' questions. He walked around until he found a quiet room with an ornate carpet that were probably hard work hard to keep clean. He sat down on a red upholstered couch against the wall and waited for the WiFi login page to finally load.

At the age of seventeen, Andrew didn't feel a call to anything. A job just seemed like an annoying thing people did to pay for rent. But even very early into his new ghost hunting gig, he started questioning things, like why the original owners of these places were so often believed to become ghosts. Was it simply an unfinished business thing, or was it a purgatory situation, and the soul had no place to go so they stayed somewhere they knew? Could ghosts not run away, or was it all a bunch of crap?

When Ryan returned, Andrew was sure they'd head up to the third floor. According to Google, that's where the former owner used to work back in the day. Instead, Ryan gestured to an exit. "Let's head out. They are more interested in their movie-related tourism right now. Want to go camping?"

"Why not? WiFi is shit here anyways." Andrew shrugged. Unconfirmed cryptid sighting it was. "Actually, could I drive?"

"Do you have a license?"

"Yeah, of course."

"Can you drive a stick shift?"

Andrew's mouth felt dry, and suddenly he wished he had put a toothbrush in his backpack. "My first crush's dad had one?"

"That experienced, huh?" Ryan laughed. "Come on, I'll teach you."

CHAPTER FIVE

As they neared the forest, a noisy grinding echoed between the trees as it cast a large jerky shadow. It wasn't just disconcerting, but terrifying, and verging on frustration for all of those involved. Ryan thought he had chipped a tooth gritting them against the SHAKE, SHAKE, STALL of the truck.

The magic spot had been a while back on the highway. The higher speed allowed for a higher gear, making the ride smoother and with less of a chance of killing the engine, over, and over. "Push the clutch back in, foot on brake, start back up." Those words had allowed the impossibility of Andrew driving correctly, for a while. A trip that should have been two hours ended up taking almost double with all of the false starts.

The truck felt like it was the wild beast they were here to investigate, as if it had literal horsepower that needed to be tamed and placated with the right movements. Coming up on the tail end of the trip, Andrew started to get a feel for it, like an intricate ritual that he still lacked the confidence to understand why certain movements worked. Andrew parked, not really in a spot, more so quickly deciding to stop before he drove into a ditch.

The pedal situation was so strange that even after they stopped, Andrew glanced down as if the brake had moved out from under his foot. "I drove a motorbike before, I thought it would translate easier."

"Yeah, every stick shift is a little different. You didn't give up though, which is commendable. I'd like to say you could tackle any stick now, but the position of the clutch pedal tends to change. But hey, maybe the grinding worked like a monster call."

"You really think?"

"I am absolutely fucking with you, kiddo."

Ryan got out of the truck and surveyed the bit of national park they ended up in. Andrew got out too, completely unsure what to make of his… well, his friend who might have the patience of a saint. There's no way his own dad would have let him try that after the second stall out, let alone the majority of the ride.

Ryan lifted his phone and nearly spun in a circle to try to find signal. "Well, my phone is useless, how about yours?"

"Uh?" He dug out his phone to check. "Looking good so far."

"I wanted to check what creatures were usually reported in the area."

"Oh, I know that. New Mexico is known for aliens." Andrew glanced around the forest, which looked absolutely natural. If someone walked deep enough in the forest, they might get a 'something watching from above' vibe. "I thought your specialty was spirits."

"When people see something they don't understand, they usually label it with whatever is most known to them. So if alien lovers see something, or the area is known for them, that's what they think. If they are really religious, demons normally come into play. Even if it's something completely normal, or literally flying. Many things come down to misidentification, like with your parents."

A twig snapped under one of their shoes and they both froze like it had been them.

"I'm sorry," Ryan said. "I guess I should have let you bring it up if you wanted."

"It's okay. It was kind of on my mind anyways." Andrew followed behind Ryan, who waited for him to continue speaking. "I mean, not in any real useful way. Just thinking."

"Yeah," Ryan seemed to agree. "That's the way of things like that. Come on, let's get a feel for the place, try to find camping areas to see if it's worth investigating at night."

"Does time of day actually matter?"

Ryan saw he was being treated as an expert, and Andrew's faith in him was encouraging. "It being darker out can make things scarier. People rely on sight, but there is such a thing as the Devil's hour. Or the witching hour, depending who you speak with. Like I said before, all of it runs into each other."

They'd been walking along a path for a good ten minutes before Andrew spoke again. He read directly off his phone. "'Psychological literature suggests that apparitional experiences and sensed presences are most common between the hours of 2 and 4 a.m., corresponding with a 3 a.m. peak in the amount of melatonin in the body.' You sure got the spirit of all that right."

"Hey look." Ryan gestured towards a building lifted up on a small hill in their sight line. "That might be something useful."

Andrew followed along, putting his phone away so he could more easily climb up. "Think anyone's just like, hey man, let's take a shit ton of melatonin and see some ghosts?"

"Oh geez, I doubt it."

What might have been a ranger's cabin at a distance ended up just being an awning that marked the entrance of a community garden. There was a plaque that explained the fees for having your own square to use. The rest of the mistaken structure was a fence to keep animals from eating the plants. The garden smelled of mint and damp earth. No one else was here, yet everything continued to silently grow without them all the same.

On their way out, Ryan pointed out a box with a small painted sign that read 'free wood'. Nailed along the side was a plastic box with campfire safety information flyers. "Let's grab some, pick a spot, and see if anything happens," Ryan said, and picked up an armful. They'd at least have to head towards the truck again to grab the fire starter.

"Mmm, this makes me kind of feel like bait."

Ryan frowned. "I'd promise there's a sign saying 'free chocolate and marshmallows' up ahead, but… a lot of ghost hunting is showing up and tempting something greater or unknown to come fuck with you."

Neon signage from a store nearby cracked a false dawn over their chosen campsite. They hadn't seen it when they picked the location, but now that it was dark enough, stars started competing for attention. Their own campfire added to the glow with a soft crackling sound and warmth that drew fingers out of pockets.

"I used to make my own constellations." Andrew connected the dots in the sky, making a trapezoid shape out of the visible dots of light. "That one was a pope."

Ryan looked up, and tried to picture the finer details. Perhaps the point was the hat, and the rest the robes.

Andrew sighed. "What kid thinks of a pope before a dragon or some shit? God, I wish my parents had been Creasters. You know, just given the option twice a year to dabble with faith. We fucking always went. Saturday morning and Sunday morning. I never got to sleep in, ever."

"You never watched Saturday morning cartoons?"

"Nah, man. They might not even be a thing now."

"What day is it?"

Andrew looked over, confused. "Uh, Friday?"

Ryan stood up. "This forest might hold a lot, but I don't sense a payday or paranormal proof that'll go viral here.

Come on, let's head back to the car. We'll find a hotel, and you can decide in the morning if you want to sleep in or watch TV."

"That's stupid." Andrew said. Ryan raised a brow that made Andrew doubt himself. "I mean silly. I—I don't know what I mean."

"Is it something you want to do?"

"Yeah, actually."

"Then it's neither of those things. Let's go. We haven't found anything, and aren't getting paid to be here." He started walking, not even realizing that Andrew wasn't following until he nearly left him behind.

"Ryan."

He turned around. "What?"

"You're like the weirdest and nicest person ever."

Ryan's smile wavered before it stuck, like he'd decided that was meant as a compliment. He pressed his lips together ready to say something when his expression shifted again into a conflicted and curious neutral, directed over Andrew's shoulder.

Andrew glanced over, trying to look where Ryan had been staring. There was no one near at eye level, so Andrew shrugged the whole thing off as the trees rustling and leaving varied shadows behind. "You should absolutely drive this time," Andrew said.

"Yeah, okay," Ryan said. He slowly started to follow, and nothing trailed behind them. At least, nothing in sight...

CHAPTER SIX

Ryan didn't know which option Andrew ended up picking. Staying somewhere that had a fixed level of light and temperature threw off his natural sleep cycle. He knew Andrew was awake because sound carried from one queen bed, over the nightstand, to another. He glanced toward it to find the time without fishing for his phone. Bit past noon. The TV was off, and Andrew was sitting on the bed with a bible open in front of him. It looked like the Gideon Bible pulled from the nightstand. Around him was nearly half a dozen pages, torn out.

Ryan didn't ask what he was doing, Andrew volunteered the information anyway, after glancing at his phone and ripping out more. "Six different verses," he said. "I saw the Bible sitting in the drawer, and it pissed me off. I wanted to tear it apart. I told myself it was stupid, or sacrilegious, or something. But then it didn't feel any more ridiculous than anything else going on lately."

Ryan did his best not to look like he was judging. He left his hands down on the blankets, keeping his eyes on the trash from the night before until he knew for sure what he wanted to say. "You know if I'm honest you're a weird kid. But you're also smart, and intuitive. They still teach who Thomas Jefferson is in school, right?"

"Where the hell are you going with this?"

"He made his own bible, and not in the 'I'm going to rewrite it to say what I want' way. He cut up the New Testament and pasted what he believed were the most important bits of Christ's philosophy. Called the new version The Life and Morals of Jesus of Nazareth. A professor of religion called it scripture by subtraction."

Andrew's expression warmed into a smile. He gathered the piles into a single pile and got up from the bed, tossing them into a small trash without any fanfare. "I'm going to get us some soda for the road."

"Sounds great." Ryan added the rest of the trash into the collection.

Ryan wasn't broke, but he was risking it if he didn't find a lead that paid again. That was just the nature of freelancing. Thankfully, check out was at two so he used the room as an office until they had to get a move on again.

Albuquerque had two haunted buildings, The Hotel Parq Central and the Kimo Theater, which also meant activity in the general area would be more likely. If Ryan could pick, it would be the latter simply because he was striking out on cold selling hotels. But it didn't matter where they went, really, as long as someone was looking for help.

He called both places. The hotel seemed confused at first, then they confirmed they didn't need anything. Performers were naturally a more superstitious bunch. Most everyone knew the saying break a leg, but people who came to the Kimo Theater also heard that they should bring a small treat or gift for a ghost of a child. When Ryan called the theater, he was transferred to the general manager after he introduced himself and what he did.

The general manager wasn't a believer. He nearly brushed Ryan off before a thought came to him. "Actually, hold on," the man said. The line went quiet for over a minute until rustling hinted at his return. "A woman called about a week ago. Real panicked, thought I might know something about how to keep ghosts away. I told her I didn't even believe in them, but she insisted I write down her information. Jane Riley." He finished the call with the number.

Ryan swiped the notepad and pen and quickly scribbled the information down.

The hotel door made a beeping sound as Andrew opened it. He juggled two bottles, the keycard, and a bag of beef jerky which must have been what took him so long. They awkwardly all ended up on the table before he dropped anything. "Have any luck?"

"Seems we are on the right track."

The right track actually brought them out to the railroad of a high-speed train that ran from Albuquerque to Santa Fe, and was painted with a roadrunner. Jane Riley lived along that path in an adobe-colonial hybrid, all tan with pale pastel trim. The only hard color came from a rose bush with white and dark pink roses reaching up towards the porch. Two dying trees framed the left side of the lot. Through the window, they could see Jane sitting, wearing a straw hat with single red flower on the brim.

She saw them before they reached the door, and opened it before they even had to knock. "Thank you for coming," she said to Ryan. She looked surprised to see a teenager in tow, but she didn't voice her thoughts. It could be a legit weekend job.

"Not a problem. We were in the area and happy to help." Ryan held his hand out to shake, and Andrew stuffed his hands in his pockets, so he didn't have to follow suit.

The inside mirrored the same style of decor as the outside. This time the splash of color was a ceramic cauldron sitting on the mantle. It was small, smaller than the palm of Ryan's hand, and glazed in a dark purple with a large white crescent moon and shooting stars dotted along the whole piece.

"Please have a seat." Jane gestured to a small dining room table. One wing hung down so the otherwise round table could be tucked against the window. Plants lined the back to soak up the sun.

"Could you tell us what sort of things have been happening?" Ryan prompted, once everyone was settled.

Jane's hands nervously clasped a mug that had already been sitting there. "It started one night when I went to bed. I woke up around two to find the house lit up. At first, I thought I had just left a light on, but I mean *everything* was on. So, half asleep, I start turning things off in the room. Lights, tv, the stereo, you name it.

"I go back asleep, and the next morning when I'm getting the mail, I said to my neighbor, 'what a weird power surge that was.' Because surely, it had to happen to the whole block. But they were confused, so I brushed off my own comment and went inside with the mail. And I stopped to realize the oven time was correct, further ruining my rational explanation," Jane continued. Her posture stooped, happy they were listening, but tired from it all. "The next night, I was woken up by a mug thrown across the room. No lights this time, but I see the shattered clay pieces on the ground. That's when I started researching, for anyone who might know how to connect those dots. Ended up calling the theater last week, knowing it was haunted, and then he gave you my information."

Ryan slowly nodded along. "Has there been anything else unusual since then?"

"No, or at least I don't know for sure. I'm real jumpy now, so any noise I think is going to be a bigger problem. But nothing that I feel provable, like those first two nights."

"Did you see or experience anything strange at the theater?"

"No, my friend just told me the rumors."

"Well," Ryan said, "I have to commend you for looking for answers so soon. Most wait, and that escalation period makes things far more stressful for you and harder to deal with in general."

Jane forced a smile, trying to be happy that she did something right. Unable to hold his gaze, she tipped her cup slightly forward, disappointed it was empty.

"Are you the only one who lives here?" Andrew asked, surprising everyone.

Jane seemed dazed at his sudden interest. "Yeah, well, just me and my dog. She's a big fluffy thing, as quiet as a mouse. She's sleeping on the bed right now."

Andrew tried to glance over, but the angle they were at didn't show them anything except a hallway of closed doors. "Did she see anything, stare or bark?" Andrew continued. Ryan watched, curious where this train of questioning was going.

Jane shook her head. "I started having her sleep in the bed with me once this started. Maybe that's why things settled down. I dunno."

Andrew put his hand to his mouth, like he knew something neither of them did.

Ryan followed up with more questions, things like whether she did any major work on the house recently, if she found anything strange, if there was any part of the house she was afraid to go into. Everything checked out.

"Are you a witch?" Andrew asked suddenly.

Ryan made a stalling noise, but Andrew's curiosity won out.

"There's a cat figure in your kitchen. Painted to match the cauldron on your mantle."

Jane's head whipped between the two spots. "Oh. I make ceramics. I have a tiny shop online and sell them as a hobby. Those two were my favorites of the batch. That was a month or more ago, though."

Ryan narrowed his eyes, wondering if Andrew thought he had solved the case. "We're happy to investigate and try to find an answer for you," Ryan said. "And either way I can bless the house."

"Thank you, that would be great." Jane stood up, and took the cup to the sink. She sighed before she turned back. "I used to go to church, but not since I was a kid. Do you think that absence caused this?"

Ryan paused, holding the question in his mind for a moment so he didn't sound dismissive. "Do you believe in God, Miss Riley?"

Her fear wasn't unreasonable. Many were taught that bad things happened because their lack of faith. It was simply unfair, since there were several verses that said it's impossible for a believer to be possessed.

Before Ryan could even recall all the related scriptures, Jane said, "Yes, of course."

"Then you needn't worry it's your fault."

She said she believed, so she did. Gatekeeping actually made people less safe by telling them they weren't allowed the faith they had. But to be fair, Ryan wouldn't have believed it was her fault even if she didn't. If he was really honest with himself, the written rules could be summarized to say: make yourself a temple and only that faith will dwell until you believe in something stronger. In his experience, that generally was true. Corruption came like a poisonous seed falling on an empty field. Shit, even Pope Francis said it was better to be an atheist than a hypocritical Catholic. *Kind of.*

"Can I pet your dog?" Andrew asked suddenly.

"Uh." Jane glanced to Ryan, who shrugged. "Sure. I'll show you the bedroom. Actually, let me give you guys a tour of the whole place. See if anything stands out to you."

The dog was just as advertised - big, fluffy, and large enough to knock a grown man over to get pets. But nothing sinister jumped out, literally or figuratively. The air also felt normal, but there'd be no way to check EMF or any other reading without the equipment.

They went outside to get just that, after sweeping the house and having Jane's dog tag along everywhere while they took their readings. As everyone settled back in the living room, the dog stole the couch, so Andrew sat on the floor as

Ryan flipped to a bookmarked page in his bible.

Jane leaned forward and touched the base of a lamp. It lit up as if by magic. She had mentioned she wasn't very spiritual, but now she looked deeply religious. Her hands together in prayer, head down, deeply believing in this moment. Ryan went from room to room, reading from the Bible with a bottle of holy water as backup. The floor creaked and footsteps vibrated through the floor before Ryan's followed behind. When the blessing finished, a gust of wind blew through the house, colder than what one would expect even if the windows had been open. They remained closed. Yet Jane's hair blew around her face before it settled back down on her shoulders.

As they left Jane's house, Ryan had the sense of being watched. He could only attribute that to Jane, even though it felt darker than that. It felt like something really had been shoved outside, and now was even more pissed for it.

Ryan packed the gear close to the side of the truck bed before he climbed into the cab. He felt a little awkward about receiving money in front of someone else, but he didn't really have much say in the matter if this road trip was to continue. "So," he said. "What do you believe just happened?"

Andrew glanced over from the passenger seat, unsure whether this was a test. "She started making things with symbols she didn't fully understand, spooked herself a little. Maybe even subconsciously. So, when the dog started demanding a share of the bed by knocking things over and misbehaving, she thought it was ghosts."

Ryan smiled as he changed gears, but said nothing.

"What? Is that not right?"

"This is one of those rare situations where it's not about what is right or not."

"When is anything not about what's right or not," Andrew said, fixing his hair with growing annoyance. "Do you really believe a random gust of air cleansed her house? That you healed it with a prayer and water droplets?"

"Hope was given to a lady so afraid at night that she

started sleeping with her dog, as if it was trained for protection. That's the important thing, and what matters. The rest… the rest is just details."

"Yeah well." Andrew scrunched down in his seat, looking at his phone. Then, with a renewed sense of teen angst, he sat up to plug it into a 12-volt adapter. "The details are how you get endless fighting over whether it's the big bang or creationism."

Ryan simply watched the road until Andrew started backtracking.

"I'm sorry, I guess it's rude to talk bad about creationism with a priest."

"No, you're fine. And it's not rude, even the Church itself says they believe in both."

"What do you know for sure?"

Andrew didn't seem to expect an answer, he was largely just going on to vent. Ryan didn't mind it. He could finally say his true feelings in front of an adult. That felt daring, stupid, and important, all at the same time.

"That I'm glad you're here," Ryan said. "It could be good for you, apart from the housing situation. That will probably grow old quick. But still, traveling can be freeing."

"Ugh. Ask to pet one dog and everyone thinks you need a mushy pep talk."

Andrew tried to keep up the bluster, but he ended up tired by the end. Maybe he did like the hopeful suggestion that something could be good, for a change.

CHAPTER SEVEN

Andrew threw a cheese puff into the air and tried to catch it in his mouth. Since he was sitting in the truck, his track record wasn't so bad, but it couldn't be described as graceful by any means.

Ryan opened the driver's door and jumped in. "Please don't get cheese puff dust embedded in the upholstery."

Andrew expected a threat of some sort to follow, designed as a "joke" that didn't feel like one. Like he'd be left to the ghosts if the car got a stain. But no "or else" came.

"You okay?" Ryan said instead.

Andrew nodded quickly. "Yeah, uh, cheese puff?"

"Nah, thanks though."

He nodded again, being sure to wipe his fingers on his jeans. "Where are we headed?"

"Out of New Mexico."

"Sweet, can't say I'll miss it."

Ryan gave his passenger an eye when traffic allowed, but

he didn't say anything more until they worked their towards the highway. "I was thinking about Tombstone, Arizona. There's a number of tiny haunted places there."

Andrew shrugged. He wasn't driving, and he really didn't have an idea of where he wanted to go besides away from where he'd been. "How far is that?"

"Um." Ryan checked against the GPS on his phone. He looked between the routes it gave with a small hum of consideration. "Six hours of driving, but we'll probably have to stop somewhere to sleep along the way."

"Tombstone is really south, isn't it?"

"Yeah."

"Maybe I'll cross the border and be free."

"Do you know Spanish?"

"Only a year's worth of it."

"Maybe you should research the idea first."

So, Andrew did... well, sort of. Not because he really had a huge desire to flee to another country, but out of boredom, and curiosity of what was possible. Literally the first Google search led him to a thread of people discussing how to do it. It was old, since the internet saved everything, but would be good for the general idea.

A couple of posts in and he was bored again. Everyone was discussing passports and retirement and neither really felt all that applicable to his situation. Besides, were people there anymore accepting? Maybe he should try California, or something. His family always talked shit about the west coast so it couldn't be all bad.

Thanks to what can only be known as internet magic, Andrew fell into a hole that somehow led him to a slideshow of banners, giant painted things miniaturized on the phone's screen. All were made with similar hues of red, yellow and blue. One said, 'Live Lobster Boy'. Another had a spider with the head of a woman. One even promised shapeshifting. He knew most of these must be fake, but he wondered if there was something real somewhere. Maybe they were the haunted houses of their time, people projecting whatever they thought was true, or what they were told about things they knew nothing about.

"Have you ever thought about doing something else? Job wise?"

It was getting dark, and it made the road ahead look all the same. Just two beams shining into the distance, as all other details around the light slowly becoming dimmer and dimmer.

"I'm not really trained to do much else," Ryan said. "I suppose I could try to join a non-denominational church, but it never felt right."

"Really? There isn't anything else you feel skilled at?"

Ryan's expression wavered. Andrew might have missed it if there had been anything else notable for miles.

"I had to take an art elective in school and actually really liked it. Even did commissions one summer. But now I'm rusty, and being an artist isn't really all that more stable. Why? Thinking of things you can do?"

"I guess. I was trying to think of what would make life interesting. Make a good story to tell people. Joining the circus probably isn't as grunge-yet-glamorous as it sounds."

"Romanticism is a hell of a drug."

They explored that theory a few hours later at a gas station tailored towards truckers inside the Arizona border. Sleeping in the back of the truck was still largely untested with the two of them, but what Andrew had not thought through was showering. When Ryan first offered, it felt like thing that would be demonically bad. Like a park bathroom, or a high school locker room, all dirty from countless people, and nearly in public.

Turns out truckers had their needs covered better. They waited around a bit, not wanting to throw a trucker off their schedule, and fashioned a dinner out of the pre-made offerings. Andrew waited, glancing down at the number he'd been given as if he'd forgotten it since the last time he checked it minutes ago.

"Weirding you out?" Ryan asked, sitting in the chair next

to him.

"I saw a sign for one of these before, but to actually use it is something else."

Ryan nodded, waiting for another customer who was just passing through to leave. "This place is smaller, but I've been to one truck stop that had a waiting room with a pool table."

"You're fucking kidding."

"Nope."

"Wow."

What had seemed like a strange new lifestyle felt pretty average after all was said and done. Andrew showered, and the word written along his thumb faded with water, soap, and the tiniest bit of encouragement, leaving him feel like a brand new person. Well not *brand* new. Maybe more like a pre-owned car that got polished up to look and feel new.

He almost wished he wasn't a minor so he could document this strange adventure for the world. YouTube stardom would have to wait, or else someone might see the video and say, 'Hey Mike and Karen, isn't that your boy?'

The truck bed was unsurprisingly less roomy when shared, but he got his pick of blanket and which direction he wanted to lie, so really it was not so bad. He definitely didn't pack correctly for this, but he could see it being done with proper planning. Just like how juggling was doable, even if he didn't feel skilled at it right now.

They made it to Tombstone Arizona before the sun rose. The rows of buildings sat with quite the wide road between them, as if in a standoff of their own. Most buildings were dim, barely lit with old fashioned looking streetlamps or the occasional lighted store window. Sitting on the right, one building glowed, as if the sun shone on it no matter the time.

"How is it possible this place both feels dangerous, and as if I could get a cowboy hat and just fuck around all day?" Andrew asked. He and Ryan both knew he was too cool to actually do the latter, but the point still stood.

"Probably picking up on both realities. A lot of people come here for a lot of reasons. Some kids only see it as a playground, others know the history, and those shoot outs - no matter how long ago - stay with them as they visit."

"Huh. Let's hunt some demons."

Ryan smiled and headed towards a sign that proclaimed rather plainly, 'Gun Fight.' Below it, wax figures cast shadows that aimed to echo what happened at the O.K. Corral. All seven figures had long coats and cowboy hats, but only the ones with guns showed any confidence. Ryan avoided walking into any of their shadows, and when Andrew noticed, he gave the ground a weary look. Ryan held his hand out at his side, as if trying to feel for figures that were not represented under the red and white painted banner over their heads.

Andrew moved to the edge of the gated area. On this side, more signs hung on the fence. He leaned his head over the short railing to see that they marked the names of each figure frozen nearby.

"Do you want to try the ghost box?" Ryan asked. He crouched low so he could easily pull equipment out of his bag.

Andrew felt almost more spooked by doing nothing. He nodded and held his hand out for the device. By this time, it had already started skipping over the radio with a scratchy wobbling sound.

"Uh, we came to ask if anyone is around that wanted to talk?" They'd been over how to use the spirit box in the car, but in person it felt different. Again, silly in that childlike and reckless way. The sun was rising against the noise, and fear rose with it. Unsure if he should say something more, or hold his breath, Andrew asked, "Did any of you survive this event?"

Ryan waited, and when no disembodied voice came, he spoke for them. "The first few died quickly, two of the survivors got ambushed. Shot in the back, one still lived after that. The gift shop has a tiny plaque marking the spot."

"Maybe that's why there's nothing." Andrew said, offering the box back. "Here that is."

Ryan gave a slight chuckle that could only be seen, rather than heard over the loud device. "If hauntings were only caused by the dead, I'd find a lot less vengeful energy around."

Andrew's mouth twitched into a smile in return, but only because he wished that had been a joke rather than the first thing he believed tonight. They ventured over to the second site, but they felt even less there.

"We should split up." Andrew's eyes went wide at the suggestion. Ryan added, "To cover more ground before the sun rises higher."

They split the gear, since having two people now meant more could be tested at once. Andrew got his pick of a simple handheld camera and flashlight. He walked down a path that brought him to a bar that still seemed in use, if not open for business right then. Carved in wood, a sign read, "WE'VE GOT FOOOD!" Saloon style doors blocked the middle of the doorway, leaving large voids of black which showed nothing of the inside.

Andrew leaned closer to the doors and heard a metal clink. Quickly pulling back, he reasoned that someone must have dropped some silverware before reminding himself that it was pitch black inside. If anyone was in there, they'd be sitting, or maybe working without any light. The thought creeped him out just as much as silverware moving on its own.

"Oh boy," he whispered to himself. A step up was hidden in the dark, and he nearly tripped through the threshold rather than confidently walking in. If whatever might be inside had been scared by his shape at the door, he doubted he seemed like a threat now. He righted his jacket. Appearing scary was probably not the best course of action anyways. Maybe a mild-mannered kid would go further.

There was some light in here after all - in a far corner, a candle sat on a table. Andrew was pulled towards it until he realized it was fake. Someone thinking, 'hey, let's not burn history to the ground' somehow did make him feel safer.

He turned, lifting the camera. "I don't know your history," he said to the air, "Maybe you'd like to share it with me?"

To say he was met with silence would be a lie. There were plenty of sounds that seemed masked enough that they had to be something else: the trilling of a bird, the building itself creaking against time or the weather. There was also a whisper he couldn't quite place. Andrew checked the tables, but they all seemed bare of any forks, spoons, knives, or glasses. High up by the ceiling was a pair of horns. He actually could see them better through the camera. Classic western decor, he thought - creepy, but not haunted.

After making his way around the room, he found a hallway covered in frames, the women's bathroom, and a door labeled as the basement. "Am I really going to try this?" he said to the camera. "Ah, fuck it. If Ryan posts it online, I'll be immortal. Hello?" he said, opening the door. "I'm Andrew."

Talking aloud didn't actually put his nerves at ease, but it was better than his thoughts only echoing around his head. As he descended the stairs, he found dozens of baby shoes on a alcove near the bottom. The ones in the front were unboxed, and to the side was a handwritten sign: Baby Shoes, $24.99. Size 1 to 5.

"Ah, yes," Andrew said, playing to the camera as he turned it around to record his face. "The true American terror. Consumerism. Come get yer basement dwelling baby shoes."

The only light downstairs came from a room blocked off by prison style bars. Andrew figured those were to keep tourists from going deeper, but even if the door was open, there were lines he wouldn't cross. But he did dare a few steps closer.

Inside was a bedroom. Without knowing the history of the place, he didn't know if at one point there was a real door or if it had always been a weird hole in the ground that made up a dungeon-slash-gift store. Further back was another passage in the wall leading off somewhere he couldn't say. The internet would probably have the answer, but he'd have to ruin this vision to check. Even if the info could reassure him, feeling his way out by hand was a tetanus shot waiting to happen.

Footsteps sounded above him. He couldn't tell whether the bar was directly above him anymore. "Ryan?" he called towards the stairs. If he had come in, surely he'd hear and call down.

Nothing. And then, a yell. Loud, but distant, calling his name. Faith that it was Ryan thinned, leaving the options either to stay in the spooky basement or to come up to find God knows what. He glanced back to the isolated dark hole. In a way it felt safer here, in this dead end between the two.

He heard his name again, a familiar tone painted with a panicked urgency, maybe even a cry for help. That stirred him to action, and he dashed up and out of the building completely.

Andrew stood on the dirt street, eyes squinting against even the calmest morning light. "Ryan?" he asked, and it soon turned into his own yell. His name wasn't shouted back.

A ringtone played, and Andrew nearly dropped everything reaching to answer his phone. "Hello?"

"Are you okay? I thought I heard you yelling."

"Yeah. Weren't you just yelling my name though?"

"No?" There was a wavering second of silence over the line. "Why would I when I could just call you?"

"Whatever," Andrew said, "Can we just meet up and leave?"

"Sure. Do you want to meet by the truck, or should I come to you first?"

"I'm by this restaurant... bar thing?" Andrew glanced back, taking a few more steps away from the door both for comfort and to see if there was a sign showing the name. Before he said anything else, Ryan said he'd meet him there in a minute.

And to his credit, he did.

"You look…" Ryan scratched at his nose. "Like you might have actually seen a ghost."

Andrew shoved his camera into Ryan's hands as they walked back to the truck. "I swear I heard someone calling my name. I thought it was you. You sure you didn't say it? Not even once?"

"I promise." One camera hung off Ryan's wrist in order to accommodate holding the second as he replayed the clip. He watched the whole thing.

They were in the car before he got to the bit in question.

"I definitely hear something, but I don't hear your name."

"You think I'm crazy then."

"Definitely not." Ryan hit rewind and watched again until he heard his own name, and then Andrew's cell phone ring. "I'm just not sure what it is. "

CHAPTER EIGHT

Despite Andrew deciding against becoming a YouTuber, the video did end up on the internet. Well, *sort of*. It was emailed to a colleague so they could get an opinion on the video without power of suggestion influencing the listener.

Andrew's thoughts on what happened changed with the mile markers. At first, he thought Ryan might be lying to scare him into believing ghosts existed. On one rewatch, he wondered if his own voice somehow had been distorted and echoed back. The only decision that stuck was that he disliked Arizona as much as New Mexico.

To be fair, their tour of roads and gas stations wasn't a stellar view. They needed gas fairly often. This time around, all the pumps were full, so Ryan parked along the side next to a dusty blue van. Andrew unbuckled his seat and glanced over. "Are you heading inside?"

Ryan's phone rang, and he went to answer. "Yeah, after this."

Andrew nodded and hopped out.

"Hey Mary," Ryan said, glancing out the truck window. "What's up?"

Mary had been ghost hunting since high school. Instead of sticking with the traditional methods, for the past forty odd years she had tested every new theory, every new piece of equipment that came out, to see its worth.

Mary got straight to business over the phone. "I don't know how to tell you my theory on what you sent."

"Okay, why? It's by far not the weirdest video I have sent you."

That title belonged to an exorcism that Ryan did. They were rarely recorded, but the paranormal group he was with insisted on it. The family didn't mind, and Ryan had been too shocked about what he was seeing to really care or try to stop them. It had gone beyond the standard church blessing, featuring a wailing believer who felt better after they had been prayed over. It had been nothing like the movies either, and yet still unexplainably unnerving. The video he sent a few hours ago was just a kid going ghost hunting and getting scared over a distant noise.

"Spit it out, Mary," Ryan said.

"I think your kid is haunted. Not in the possessed sort of way, and not quite in the attachment fashion either. The first time I heard the video I thought it was fake. I thought he added the sounds himself in post. The voice pattern looks like his, but pitched in a way that suggests software, or... age."

Ryan rolled his eyes, and craned his chin up with a shake. "You think he is his own ghost?"

"Look, I get it sounds outlandish. But in times of great change sometimes people reach out to themselves, especially those who tend to hang around areas full of energy. The brain is a complex thing, and can do inexplicable things."

"So what? No other theories than his future self is

haunting him?" Ryan's free hand gripped the wheel. The leather creaked under the pressure.

"I hadn't speculated on age," Mary corrected. "I check EVPs all the time. Most are caught after playing the video back. Ones that are caught in the moment usually are assumed to be whatever the asker wants, so if someone asks, 'what color shirt am I wearing,' they will usually hear a color. If they hear anything at all. I heard the name, but that doesn't mean that's what was said. The sound was unprompted. If he had asked what his name was then got the sound, I'd list it as a Class A EVP. There's only been a few of those that can't be debunked. Given the context of everything, well... you have my theory."

Ryan sighed, rubbing the slight stubble on his chin. "Okay, thank you for looking at it so fast."

"Take care, Ryan."

He looked down at the phone until the screen turned off. Ignoring this whole conversation felt like it would be easier, but hiding away information never felt right. He didn't want to be one of those adults who claimed they'd explain when someone was older.

A look in the rear mirror showed that a pump was open, so Ryan shifted the truck into reverse and maneuvered around to fill up. He gathered any trash and tossed it before running out of things to procrastinate with and headed inside to find Andrew.

"That was my contact who called," he said. "Do you want to know her wild theory?"

Andrew was glancing over the clearance section, doing the math on whether anything in the pile of bagged treats was better than a 2 for $3 sale he found. The question caused him to turn away. "Why not? Hit me."

"Do you know what a siren is?"

"Those mermaids who sing?"

"Kind of. They sing things people really want, doesn't matter what it is." Ryan could tell by the look on Andrew's face that he had no idea where this was going. "Let me try to explain another way. You know how some people have deeply negative thoughts towards themselves? The reverse can be true. That intuition can actually be a warning system. And some, like my contact, believe if enough energy is around, those thoughts can become audible. She thinks the voice you heard was you."

"What the fuck. I thought this 'a demon ate my son' bullshit was over."

"It is," Ryan said. "From a Bible standpoint, there are many stories of angels coming to people with messages. Guiding them. And I've sensed something every time we go somewhere. It could be possible that your guardian angel could be you."

"This is so fucking weird. I just..." Andrew tossed his hands in the air. "I'm going to go for a bit. Get lunch or fucking something."

Ryan nodded. He thought about leaving it there, but he simply couldn't. "At the end of the day," he said, "it's about what you want to believe. That's the truth about yourself."

Andrew nodded. He swayed a little before he committed to walking away. Ryan was worried, but he wasn't his father, and legally he couldn't do a thing if Andrew decided to run away from him like he did his parents. All he could really do was wait here long enough to give Andrew a chance to come back if he wished. And if he didn't, at least it wouldn't be on Ryan's conscience that he gave up too soon.

Andrew found Ryan sitting in the booth at the connected fast food place. All that was left of Ryan's food was a tray of wrappers that were mostly to show that he'd been a customer. His cup had been refilled twice already by the time Andrew returned, as if he had casually gone to the bathroom.

"Let's say," Andrew said, "hypothetically, that I was trying to give myself a message. What did, I dunno, I want?"

Ryan leaned forward, rubbing one of his eyes. "I was

thinking about it, and about how people say they have a calling. That they are pulled to do a thing, that it speaks to them. Normally they mean a profession or passion. And it makes me sound like a youth pastor, but fuck, it would fit."

Andrew snorted. "I'm not sure what that even means. Like, what am I supposed to do? Go to college with your ghost hunting money? Find a job? Be someone in society?"

"Just be... who you needed when you were younger." Ryan pressed his lips together before leaning forward. "I'm not under any illusion that I'm here to save you. And I don't think any priest directly does that in the first place. But I do believe that people help each other. And that there's an inner voice trying to tell us the truth about ourselves."

They stared at each other, unsure if anything else should be said.

"Did you want to go to college?" Ryan asked.

"Not really." Andrew shrugged. "It's one of those things I thought I was meant to want. Like girls. But I never started to actually want it. I teamed up with you because I didn't know what I wanted, and you seemed like a safe bet. And I guess I still don't know what I want, but I feel like it's better than..." His eyes looked around the room without solid focus. "It's better than standing in the dark, putting up with 'protection' that was just slowly suffocating me."

"I get that." Ryan nodded. "I really do." He smiled.

"What?"

"Teamed up." Ryan smiled more freely. "I like that."

Andrew leaned back in the booth. "I have a few questions first."

Ryan mirrored him in his seat. If the questions weren't a trick, maybe he should get settled first. "Okay."

"What would you have done if I had been possessed, or had an attachment, or whatever the fuck TV ghost hunters call it these days."

"Exorcised you," Ryan answered. Judging by his face, it was far too simple an answer for Andrew to buy it. "I don't understand the look. This all might seem like a weird road trip to you, but it's what I was trained to do."

"Okay, fine. Ask me a question," Andrew said.

Ryan squinted, trying to think of anything to ask. He settled on, "What would you do if I was the one possessed? Like if we were out on a hunt, split up, and you found me just standing in the corner, staring."

Andrew scoffed. "Leave your ass behind."

Ryan laughed. "That's a good survival instinct."

"What if there's a zombie invasion, got a plan for that?"

"Okay, full disclosure, neither of those things are going to happen."

There was a slight shake of his head before Andrew went on, "Okay, what's *actually* comes next?"

Ryan leaned over in the seat, reaching for his bag. He pulled a paper map out of the pocket and laid it out on the table, pressing the creases down. "I assume you want to avoid any more ghost towns with mining backgrounds that have creepy holes in the ground."

"Would be preferable, yes."

"So, I was looking up some stuff earlier, and there's a bunch of stuff around." He leaned over again, this time to grab a pen. He made a little X over seven different cities. "Someone online already made a road trip map of all ghost towns nearby. If we exclude the mining towns, that leaves us..." Ryan's voice trailed off, trying to remember his history to see what was left. "Fairbank is nearby. Old railroad town. Or you could say eff Southern Arizona, and we could go to Flagstaff—"

"Fuck Southern Arizona."

"Hear me out first. Flagstaff has a hotel with literally a dozen reported ghosts."

"And?"

"It is at least a five-hour drive."

"So? You must've brought it up because you thought it was reasonable." Andrew rubbed the back of his neck. "Does it have a better chance of being paid or something?"

"Probably, since it's a bigger city. I also know Flagstaff

better. If you wanted to stay somewhere, it definitely isn't the worst place."

"Why do you like it?"

Ryan gaze grew unfocused. "First place I saw snow."

Andrew had self-elected himself to pick up Ryan's food tray, and started to scoot out to toss it. In passing he asked, "Really?"

"Yeah, why?"

With a tilt, he poured all of the trash into the can. "I dunno, expected something... more. Maybe something less naturally whimsical."

"Should I take it that's where you decided we are going?"

"Guess so."

"Here then." Ryan tossed Andrew the keys. He had to scramble to catch them. Then he had to scramble a little more to make sure the trash didn't intercept them as he fumbled. Once the keys were secure, Ryan went on. "You picked the location, so you might as well drive."

This time driving wasn't a jerky, grinding horror story. Their main fear was running out of gas near the end of the trip. The tank got about 330 miles per tank, so given that the trip itself was about 328 miles, the two rolled into town on fumes.

The Hotel Monte Vista had a sign suspended several feet in the air by a small network of scaffolding. At night it glowed like any other sign, but in the day, it popped out over the building, adding 3D in an already three-dimensional world.

The inside of the building was like a golden box. Yellow lights bounced around reflective surfaces, making the place glow. Mary stood in the lobby, her black skin catching the light in an even better way. She pulled her hands from her puffer jacket to offer Ryan into a hug as they walked in.

"So excited to see you again." She smiled, then she turned towards Andrew. "And you are the kid from the video, right?"

Ryan knew that in Andrew's head, this lady had been an asshole, but given a day of driving and some thought he didn't seem to think she was so bad. Just the bearer of bad news. Andrew pulled on a friendly expression. "That's me."

She gave him an extra curious look. The smile slipped off Andrew's face.

With the grace of a tour guide, Mary moved on. "So," she said, "I'm glad you let me hook you up here. I've already booked the most haunted room in the place. Room 305, but another haunted room, 220, is free tonight, so we can investigate there too. I got a ton of new equipment to test out." She patted the side of a large messenger bag.

"What's the theory this time?" Ryan asked.

"I've been working with the effects of electricity in active and inactive areas, trying to see if adding or removing power can help summon paranormal activity. Shall we head up to the room?"

The boys followed Mary up to 305. An old wooden rocking chair sat under a mounted television in a pea green painted room. The color was overwhelming, even though it matched the aging regal style of the room. Mary gingerly placed the bag on the queen bed and started unpacking it.

"Damn," Andrew said, watching Mary pull a dozen or so power banks out, "it looks like a Best Buy in there." She sat each bank next to their corresponding cords.

"I'm most excited to get this baby to work," Mary said. Carefully, she lifted a palm sized pad with a black wire trailing off it. "It's a charging pad. My theory is it will work even better than asking a ghost to directly drain the camera's battery. Can you plug it in for me, Andrew?"

"Uh, okay." He carefully took it from her, treating it with extra care. "Where did you want it?"

"Wherever you think is best. I have plenty of extension cords, so don't worry about not finding an outlet."

Andrew glanced around the room, with no idea of where this thing should go. He wavered between a spot by the window and a spot by the chair, but since there was a plug by the chair that location won.

Ryan quietly set up camera equipment without any

direction, like he had several other times when haunting ghosts with Mary in the past. She always had an idea of what to try, so Ryan easily found himself following her lead. By the time the room was set up, the place was wired. So much electricity was being pulled from several sources that the that the room almost vibrated with it all.

"Perfect," Mary declared. "Let's check out room 220 before it gets too late. Everyone grab some equipment."

On their way down a floor, Mary explained the strange history of the room. The ghost believed to reside there allegedly had the odd quirk of hanging raw meat from the chandelier when he was alive. The "Meat Man" died in the room, and was known for cold hands and messing with the television. As visual as hanging raw meat would have been, Mary was particularly interested in the TV misbehaving.

The Meat Man's room was painted in a cream color, with an old wood door that didn't match the richer wood of a dresser inside. The bed was bookended by two nightstands. Lamps and a single mirror hung on the wall next to the bed.

Before they even fully set up, there was knocking - seven little raps that seemed to be coming from the closet. Ryan's camera caught it, as well as a slightly off-guard Andrew and Mary. She reached her hand out, fingers moving just so, as if feeling the air for a spider's web.

"Are you happy that we are here?" she asked.

They heard another knock, or maybe the sound of footsteps in the hall. She hummed approvingly.

The noise shifted away as Mary opened the closet. "Are you in need of some rest?" she asked, listening for the knocks. "If you're overwhelmed with energy there's a dead battery here." She reached into her pocket and pulled out a thin cylinder-shaped power pack. With a careful, slow-motion flourish of someone dealing with police, she placed it on the table. "Are you still there?"

This time the question was met with silence. Mary gave it another moment before starting with a new question but before she finished, Ryan interrupted.

"My battery died."

Mary looked over to her shoulder at him. When she spoke, a slight accent came out. "Really?"

"Was at 72%, then nothing." Ryan tried to turn the camera back on again, but it was useless.

Andrew walked closer, giving the camera a funny look before digging around in his own supplies. "Here's the spare."

"May I have the dead one?" Mary asked.

Ryan handed it over before loading the camera with its replacement. This time the camera turned on, and the display showed the battery was at 88%. "Much better."

"I thought batteries were meant to do better in colder areas?" Andrew asked. "I swear that was full."

"They are." Mary placed the second empty battery next to the first like an offering. "I'm going to turn the lights off, okay?" Whether she was asking them or the ghost, no one answered before the lights turned off.

Only Ryan could really see with the camera's night version turned on. The other two just sat down in the dark, Mary on the bed, and Andrew on the floor. He glanced at the dark glass of the mirror and tugged at Ryan's pant leg for him to look. There was a little glow there. He thought it was reflecting a light from the street before he remembered they weren't on ground level.

"Hey, Mary," Andrew said softly, before worrying he'd be mistaken as a disembodied voice. "I think a light on your powerpack turned on."

Mary tilted her head, leaning forward on the bed to get a better look. A squeak of the springs echoed her movement. "I think it's the charge indicator. When there's three it means it's full. Let's leave them there, if it's okay with you, Ryan. We can later come back to see if anything has changed."

"That's fine." Ryan changed settings on the camera, and a small light on the front turned on to show their way out. Andrew blinked at the hallway lights. They were naturally dim, but like a sun in comparison to the dark room.

"I'm going to check out the basement," Mary declared with a gesture towards the elevator.

"I'd like to check on the first room again," Ryan said, "and grab a *spare* spare battery."

Andrew didn't need more than a second to decide basements were a new no-go zone for him. "Upstairs it is," he said. As he followed Ryan into the second elevator, he asked, "So who, or what I guess, is believed to be in 305?"

"An old lady who used to be a long-term renter of the room," Ryan said. "People say she would just sit at the window, rocking. But since this is often considered the most haunted place in Arizona, everywhere in this hotel has its own story. There's even a tale about a ghost elevator attendant who asks what floor you want while he closes the gate."

"Oh, wow."

Andrew gave the mirror inside the elevator a quick look, as if he was warning their reflections to be on their best behavior. Ryan felt a tightness in his chest, but remained silent.

They got out, and Ryan pulled out the room key to unlock it. The room was as empty as when they left it, besides the slowly moving rocking chair.

The two of them didn't move in from outside of the door. They watched the chair very slowly lean forward once more, then back to balance itself, still as if it hadn't been moving at all.

"You saw that, right?" Andrew asked.

"I did." Ryan took the first step forward, giving the chair as much room as he could in the limited space. He checked the stationary camera that had been set up in the room to check and see if it, too, had seen the rocking chair move. "Come here a second."

Andrew shut the door behind them as Ryan beckoned him closer. "Was it recorded?"

"Camera stayed running, at least." He hit play.

Shortly after they left, the chair had started to sway. Nothing grand, but a soft, almost idle motion that only just stopped when the door opened again.

"What could it be?" Andrew asked. "Air pressure?"

Ryan puffed his cheeks out, wishing he had an answer. Instead, he slowly shrugged.

Andrew walked back over to the door and opened and closed it to see if he could get to the chair to move. When it refused to cooperate, he gave the chair a dirty look before sitting down on the far side of the bed. "If we are allowed to sleep here with Mary tonight, I'm still picking the truck. Punk ass chair."

Ryan grinned, barely holding back his amusement as he grabbed the spare battery he'd come in for.

"'Place is definitely haunted,'" Andrew said. It took Ryan half a second to sort out that he was reading off his phone instead of just declaring his belief to the room. "'Our bathroom door kept opening and creaking. Nice if you're into that stuff. Four out of five.' 'Somewhat haunted, we enjoyed the bar up front. Three stars for value, four for everything else.' Oh, here's a five-star review. 'Charming. While I don't believe it is haunted, it is fun to pretend.'"

"So, from what I understand here," Ryan said, "the ghosts are costing the hotel a star."

"Uh." Andrew started to scroll a bit faster. "Yeah, seems like it."

"Isaiah 43:26. 'Review the past for me, let us argue the matter together.'"

CHAPTER NINE

Flagstaff served as a background for several days before they were actually requested somewhere else. Each night stringed together a growing ease as Ryan and Andrew got the hang of traveling together. The name of the town they were in now was unknown, but between the two of them, they might be able to figure out which state they were in.

"Hey, hey, stop the car," Andrew said. He started to lean out of his seat.

Ryan slowed, but he didn't know exactly where he was meant to go. With a squint, he made out a sign. "At an estate sale?"

"Yeah, can we? Something caught my eye."

"Why not," Ryan said. He pulled up behind another car along the curb. The estate was a townhouse which had some stuff piled up on the driveway. The front door was open, and people were coming and going casually looking at their finds on the way out.

Ryan followed as Andrew made a beeline to a table, knowing exactly what he wanted. In the middle of the wares, standing on all fours, was a cat. At a distance, Ryan thought it was a pet walking through all the stuff, but he quickly realized it was something even more wild. The four long legs and paws were polka dotted, the torso striped with black and yellow. It looked like it would feel like a stuffed animal, even though they hadn't ventured a squeeze to confirm. The cat's face was the most normal thing about it, and a strong juxtaposition from the black tail that had a matching black and yellow lamp shade on it.

"I love it," Andrew declared.

Ryan laughed, clearly less convinced. "We have nowhere to put it."

Andrew picked it up off the table. He wasn't hugging it to his chest, but it was clear he was smitten all the same. "But it can be our mascot."

"I'm going to look inside while you think of a name for them."

"Them. Them is right," Andrew agreed. His focus never left the cat. "It's clearly divine and otherworldly."

Ryan thought about the landscaping, wondering how much longer the manicured hedges were going to stay that way. Perhaps the insides of the building were being sold off and the shell upkept to be placed on the market. A woman just inside the door greeted every newcomer, noting that everything inside was for sale except the vehicles in the garage. The floor had been recently waxed, likely to someone's chagrin since all the strangers would ruin the polish by the end of the sale.

The truck could hold anything they wanted, but that space was needed for them to sleep, so any impulse buys would have to stay on the small size. Ryan had wandered into the bedroom by time Andrew walked in, cat lamp under his arm so his thumbs were free to text.

"You found me quick for not looking up."

Andrew continued to text, which seemed to prove Ryan's

point. "I asked the front door lady."

"Ah."

Two other people were in the room, going through a standing jewelry box. One had several chains looped around their hand, holding them as their friend continued to look. They had pulled something far bigger than a necklace out, and they were having trouble putting it back. In the end, they left it on the bottom lip of the mirrored case before they headed out of the room.

"Have you ever thought about getting a traditional mattress for the truck?" Andrew asked.

Curiosity led Ryan over to the jewelry collection. He crouched down. "Tried it once, but most mattresses are too thick, and I lost a lot of head room."

"Oh yeah, that would be awful."

The discarded piece of jewelry wasn't jewelry at all. It was a thick metal cross about four, maybe five inches long. There was a small loop on the top as if a chain could be placed on it, but it would have been far too heavy for that. Ryan messed with the loop until it unscrewed. The top half slid away to the left. Inside was a separate cross all together, thin and wooden, at the joint sat a darker piece of wood.

Andrew craned his head forward, trying to see. "What did you find?"

"I think it's a reliquary."

"A what?"

Ryan turned so Andrew could actually see what he was holding. "A reliquary holds holy objects. You usually see them as gold standing pieces where the object hangs inside for viewing." This cross was definitely not gold. It looked like aged brass, maybe. A crucified Jesus figure was mounted on the front by his hands and feet against a black inset. "Small ones like this are usually personal objects belonging to priests, nuns, maybe the family of a church official."

"Huh, what are the odds?"

Andrew set the lamp down for a moment so he could hold his hand out to see further. When Ryan dropped it in his hand, he was surprised by the weight.

"Catholic reliquaries like this are usually believed to have a piece of the true cross," Ryan said.

"True cross?" Andrew's eyes widened. He looked like he almost didn't want to hold it anymore, but he had too much reserve to simply drop it, even if it would have only fallen on the bed. "Like… like the actual original cross?"

Andrew found the nerve to push it open again, but he seemed lost about which piece of the wood was the holy bit. Ryan assumed it had to be the tiny piece in the center, otherwise it seemed too large for an ancient thing. But then again, an object from a millennium ago carved into splinters and passed out to the faithful didn't make him feel better either.

"Are you getting it?" Andrew asked.

Ryan took it back, tightening the loop on top and spinning the INRI inscription under his finger. "Might as well see how much they want."

"It's much creepier than my lamp."

"You say that now. Wait until you wake up and feel like that thing is staring at you."

"Doubt it." Andrew lovingly picked up his cat lamp. "Their name is Frank."

"Is it now?" Ryan laughed. "That's a solid name."

They walked around the rest of the house, and as their last purchase, they picked up a puzzle. It wouldn't be too large, only 275 pieces, but it would help kill time in the back of the truck.

The same lady who'd been manning the door was selling something to an elderly man. With the possible holy relic, the lamp, and a puzzle that even promised 'Easy Handling' on the lid, they waited in line like she was a proper cashier.

"Hello again. How much for these two things?" Ryan held out his palm with the cross in it and gestured towards Andrew's lamp.

She blinked at the cat, but reeled her surprise in. "That cross," she said, "has been with the owner for many decades.

It was blessed during one of their trips overseas."

Ryan nodded as if this was very helpful information. All it meant to him was that it was incredibly bad form for a good Catholic to sell blessed things. He had to assume she didn't know that, and that the owner hadn't intended to ever sell it.

"How's 300 sound?" She made it sound like she was offering a deal. To be honest, Ryan didn't know if that was highway robbery or the steal of a century. Still, he had only ever seen one like this before, and he felt he'd regret leaving it.

"Can you throw the cat and puzzle in?"

In truth, it was possible the cat lamp was worth more. It looked like it either belonged in a kid's room, or in a modern art museum.

She glanced over again, this time looking at the cat longer. Her smile grew a little. "Sure."

With the cross and their new mascot in tow, they hit the road again. Ryan offered Andrew a chance to drive again, this time because he actually wanted a break, but Andrew's phone was very popular today, so he passed.

"Heh, look at this," Andrew said, about an hour in. He held up his phone to show Ryan an emoji that wasn't like any emoji he had ever seen before. There was a halo on top and a blue gradient transitioned to the bright yellow of most emoji faces. Four dots made up the eyes, and there was a total of three hands. Two were palm open on each side and a third was in the middle, shushing and large enough that it rose in between both sets of eyes.

"Good gosh, give that thing some wings and you have a seraphim. What is that emoji even meant to mean?"

"Someone made a site where you can make your own by mixing them together. My friend sent me this cap." He turned his phone back, clearing a new message. "That one was called 'BE NOT AFRAID.'"

"Did you raise your voice because it's all in caps, or for effect?"

"It's honestly all in caps."

Ryan laughed. "Well, thank you."

They stopped at an RV park and set up an extension cord running out of the camper's window so Frank, the cat lamp, could help them with the puzzle.

Several piles were vaguely laid out into wings, eyes, background, and edge pieces. Ryan was doing the lion's share of the owl puzzle while Andrew took plenty of text breaks.

"Who are you talking to?" Ryan asked as he finished placing the last corner piece down.

"Remember how you told me to work on figuring out what my calling was?"

"Yeah?"

"I'm working on that."

Ryan picked up a piece before pausing. "Can I know the details?"

"Not yet." When Andrew looked up, he was grinning.

"Keep your secrets then," Ryan teased. "But don't hoard the background bits. I think you have some of the wing pieces."

The middle of the puzzle proved to be the trickiest. The obvious pieces were placed and what they knew about the middle floated there in small clumps. The two ended up staying up longer than they had planned, compelled to finish.

"Fuck'n shit," Andrew grumbled as he overlooked a nearly complete picture. Ryan didn't reply as he searched the box and the surrounding area for the piece that would click into the background and complete the chest of the bird.

"Yep," Ryan said. "We are absolutely missing a piece."

CHAPTER TEN

It took a few days of back and forth emailing and texting, but Andrew found a time that would suit everyone.

To be fair, *everyone* was over-selling it. Andrew had picked a time and place that suited him, and Ryan, by proxy of sharing the truck. Andrew hadn't fully told him what his plan was, or who they were meeting up with, simply that there was a Christian family that needed help. He sold the idea as less of a demon problem with a lot of selective comments that were said with enough earnestness that Ryan agreed to drive.

The trip was slow at first. It took a little over six hours, but it felt like more, driving miles over endless desert landscapes that hadn't really changed since leaving Flagstaff. A little after crossing into California, the color green started showing up again, refusing to be forgotten.

One-thirty was an odd time for Monday church service, but Ryan didn't think too much of it as he walked up to a white building nestled in by a bunch of retail buildings. In some ways, it was better that certain branches of Christianity did this - renting out a building and making it their spiritual home - but for as much as Ryan could see the merits and freedom of that, it still felt strange as well.

The question of whether this was for mass or not was answered when they stepped inside and it became clear that the full parking lot hadn't been gathered to pray. At least, not in a traditional sense. They were here for a concert. The stage had a four-member family band performing - the parents, he assumed, and their two kids which were apart by at least several grades.

The eldest was a daughter, and the star. She could have even been that shining and immortal Christmas Star lighting the way. Ryan and Andrew didn't get far into the room before stopping to watch, for more reasons than it being a packed room. Her voice made the place feel as if it was full of flashing lights, as if she sang just for you.

Beneath the angelic lead's sweetness was something more sinister. The rest of the family wasn't without talent, but their names would never be in lights unless they all stuck together under their surname. If she had written a word across her hand it would have been 'ardent.' Passionate, glowing. But she didn't seem like the type to rebel by scribbling on herself, or at least, this scripted innocence didn't seem to have room for it.

The lyrics verged on a fantasy that wasn't about Christ, a love that wasn't about feeling blessed, but about being a vessel for "the spirit." The lyrics almost had the pornographic innocence of Marilyn Monroe. Only almost, of course.

But when Ryan listened, even for a moment, he was instantly swept up in that voice. In the middle of the song, she opened up her eyes, and all those imaginary flashing lights could have burst into fireflies as she sang for the pure love of it. The whole thing sounded like a prayer.

Three more songs later, the show wrapped up, and the audience began shuffling around to their next task. Ryan leaned into Andrew, who still seemed transfixed by the singer. "Are we are meeting up with the parents? What's the plan?"

Andrew quickly checked his phone and exhaled roughly. "I was hoping to catch just Rebecca, but the whole family seems to be busy right now."

"Rebecca. Is that the girl?"

"Yeah. She's an adult, though. Mom's name is Sarah."

Ryan nodded like he understood, but he didn't. In their fucked-up society, he knew that meant "legal", but Andrew was a minor and gay. Bringing it up didn't make sense, and it reminded Ryan of the creepy fact that her appearance was designed to trend towards youth.

Andrew tried to wave down Rebecca, but he had some trouble thanks to fans gathering as she helped her family pack their instruments up.

"Damn it. I see why she originally planned to meet us after."

Ryan silently tagged along as Andrew walked, glancing at posters that advertised today's concert: 'The G Gibson Family Band, featuring Rebecca Grace.'

"She?" Ryan repeated. The short sound oddly hung in the air until Andrew looked over. "Why does it feel like we are for *her*, rather than here to help the family?"

Andrew ran a hand through his hair as he stalled for time. A better time to explain would have been the whole drive here, rather than now. Rather than backpedaling, Andrew tried flattery: "Because you are very perceptive when it comes to the matters of Christ and his followers?"

Ryan shook his head. "Oh, Lord."

"It's fine, it's fine," Andrew said, holding up his hands. "We just came a little early."

Ryan held his tongue for a moment and blinked. They did indeed seem destined to wait. "Perfect amount of time for you to tell me the whole plan."

Andrew glanced over his shoulder. Whatever sign he was looking for didn't seem there. "Twenty minutes. You were kind enough to wait this long, just twenty more and I'll tell you everything."

Sensing trouble, but not sure from where, Ryan agreed. *Ish.* "Yeah, I'm going to wait by the car."

"If you see a Beetle with a sunroof, that's hers. It's red like Ray."

Ryan wasn't sure if he wanted that bit of information or not, but he nodded all the same. He walked back out to the truck and sat in the driver's seat. Sitting in the back sounded like it would invite possible conversation. He hadn't planned on even looking for the Bug, but from the cab, he could see the nose of one between two silver cars.

He waited twenty minutes, but Andrew didn't show up. With half curiosity and half boredom, Ryan got out of the car and walked across the parking lot to the Beetle. In the bottom corner of the window was a removable sticker. Along the sides, the sticker said 'resident' in all white against a dark blue background. In the middle were two trees and the words 'Spanish Palms.' It was close to where he had lived in Florida. Ryan tried to guess the odds of seeing that here, on the car belonging to the person they drove to meet as he walked around to the back. It had California plates, and the registration stickers were stacked at least three high, adding to the puzzle that was becoming Rebecca Grace Gibson.

Meanwhile, Andrew's plan for today had shifted into overdrive. The plan had been vague to start, amounting to a meet and greet style visit for a friend off the internet. This felt like rescuing a princess that hadn't packed yet.

"Hold up," Andrew said. "I haven't even told Ryan yet."

Rebecca stopped solid, all her movement crashing into a stillness that slowly grew like a live orchestra. "We've been talking for a couple of weeks," she said. "You weren't even in this state until this morning, and you are telling me you didn't even get an all clear?"

"Technically, you are absolutely right but..." Andrew held out a finger, ready to give an explanation that would fix everything. He had nothing. With a sigh, his hands dropped. "Okay, look, I didn't tell him because I thought he might say no. You know, there's not really a lot of room to split another way."

Halfway through, Rebecca started talking to herself. "Great. Fudging great. My escape plan is ruined. Guess I'll have to steal my—"

"Come on, listen to me. I knew, I just knew he wouldn't be able to say no if he saw you were in need. He just has to meet you beforehand, like he did with me."

Rebecca looked him in the eyes. "Are you absolutely, extraordinarily, positive?"

"You sound like Mary Poppins when you do that," Andrew said. "I'm absolutely fucking sure."

"Cool, cool. That's really great... because I also didn't tell you a few details." Rebecca's hands tightened on the straps of the guitar over her shoulder. "I didn't tell my parents I wanted out of the band. Because I don't, and it's complicated, and I was kind of hoping we could settle it, like a hundred miles away."

"Holy shit!"

Andrew attempted to pull himself together, pretending it didn't matter. Maybe if he believed it didn't, it wouldn't.

"Whatever," he said. "Ryan is already waiting."

Andrew expected to meet at the truck, and his feet shuffled to a stop as they found Ryan standing at the Beetle.

"Okay so, confession time. This is Rebecca, she recently broke up with her girlfriend–"

"Secret girlfriend," Rebecca added.

"She recently broke up with her *secret* girlfriend, right before this big family concert, and now would like to run away with us. Please?"

Andrew smiled, aiming for puppy dog eyes through his mountain of anxiety. If Ryan said no, he would stay to keep the promise made to Rebecca, even though he'd completely come off as a homeless bad boy who wanted to corrupt a sweet, innocent, "straight" lead singer.

"Back up," Ryan said. The teens blinked at each other as Ryan pinched the bridge of his nose. "Girl who is friend, or formally dating?"

"Dating," Rebecca said, sounding almost guilty. She probably hadn't quite gotten over the fact that it was an okay thing to say. Andrew understood.

"This is your car, is it not?" Ryan asked Rebecca nodded, sweat beading on her forehead. Ryan shrugged. "Why don't you just drive out of town?"

"I love this car with my whole heart," Rebecca said. "I got it for my sixteenth birthday, and thought I had the greatest life in the world. Budding stardom, the car of my dreams... and then I met Abigail. I don't want to hide shit like that for money, and I know if I stay with my family I'll have to. Out of guilt, if nothing else. Since the car is in their name, keeping it is a package deal."

Ryan looked at her for a moment. Wordless for long enough for Andrew to stop and wonder if Rebecca's thoughts ever matched his. If she ever felt the need to laugh it all as if it was a joke. *Haha, that's not my life. My life is perfect. Jk, bye!*

"Okay," Ryan said.

"Really?"

"You can come with us, but we should make this quick. If you are going to be missed, then we can't be spotted or it risks Andrew being here. You're an adult and can do whatever you want. Andrew legally can't."

"I know. That's why I packed a bag and hid it in my trunk." She popped open the back of her Beetle and pulled out a black bag, slinging it over the shoulder that didn't have the guitar. "One more second." She moved to the front to peel off the decal from Florida.

"Ready?" Ryan asked.

Rebecca tossed the keys in and closed the door. She took a deep breath, not looking at either of the boys, before she turned to them with a sure to be award winning smile someday.

"Ready."

CHAPTER ELEVEN

Figuring out what was for dinner was easy: Pizza. They ordered it for pick up and then drove to a nearby park. It was a patch of grass that took up three or four lots, with multiple covered tables, a jungle gym in the corner, and bathrooms that weren't the things of horror stories.

"You're so bad at cussing," Andrew said, laughing through a mouthful of breadsticks. "I bet you can't even flip me off properly."

"What do you mean?" Rebecca asked.

"Like your goodie-two-shoes hand won't let you."

"It would be an honor to flip you off." She turned her hand up and gave him the middle finger. The gesture looked unpracticed, but she had it for the most part.

"Miracles do happen."

"Probably from the guitar playing," Ryan chimed in.

Rebecca half shrugged; half nodded in agreement.

Ryan wanted this to be a good night, a happy one, that she

could think back on as a moment where she knew life would be okay. Still, he had questions.

"I hate to be too serious, but there's an elephant in the room I gotta mention. You may have given up your chance at a career that could have taken you anywhere."

Rebecca put down her slice of pizza on the corner of the open lid. "I can sing anywhere. That's what I love, the rest… it was always just extra to me. Like those breadsticks. I'm glad we got them, but they aren't a meal on their own."

"Speak for yourself," Andrew said, picking up another.

Ryan smiled, deciding that at least this part of the night was what he was hoping for.

When it came to the logistical side of there now being three of them, things started to break down a little. After dinner, they set out on a quest for three sleeping bags. That way, they could have warmth and leg room without needing to worry about stealing each other's blanket. Even with their best efforts, they knew it wasn't ideal. When morning came, they were all too tired to complain about something they agreed on. Plus, it wasn't a completely rotten morning. They had cold pizza for breakfast after all, and they decided not to debate the legality of Rebecca taking a nap in the bed of the truck as they drove her to her first ghost hunt.

According to the Quakers, any two or more people gathered together to talk about God was called a meeting, which acted in place of "traditional" church services. Their goal was to discuss God when moved to, and what the trio was currently debating *might* have counted.

It might also have been something else completely.

"You know how some vampires can't say God's name?" Rebecca asked.

"Right?" Andrew said, tentatively agreeing. To be fair to himself, it was an odd prompt, and he was partially distracted as they wandered around the house. Its owner had given them the keys and vowed to stay away for the night while they investigated. Rebecca seemed to assume this was the usual for the boys, but Andrew enjoyed finally investigating a house that was still being lived in. It felt more alive than the historical sites, which felt dim in comparison.

Metaphorically, that is, since the lights were off. There was a tapping down the hall, and with a quick questioning look to each other, the teens allowed their feet to guide them towards it.

"Hear me out," Rebecca continued. "What if someone was turned into a vampire and found out they shared their name with God?"

"I'm not sure I follow," Andrew said. "So just like, some vampire named like Greg or what-the-fuck-ever tries to introduce himself after he'd been turned, finds himself tongue tied, and in horror he realizes that the OG God is also named Greg?"

"Exactly."

The tapping noise subsided after they entered the room. If anything, only a scarce echo of it remained, at least to their ears.

Andrew shrugged. "Checks out to me."

They consulted Ryan, who was in the hall and serving as the bible referee for all the hypothetical examinations of big-G God they threw around.

"There are no vampires in the Bible."

This hadn't been the first round, more an interrupted version of a game they were playing that they picked back up once it was just the three of them again. He didn't think the homeowners would enjoy the off-topic discussion, but they weren't here. Besides, it wasn't like demons vanished at a hypothetical, and he doubted ghosts did either.

The only thing out of the ordinary about the house was the abundance of smart tech. Before meeting Mary, Andrew wouldn't have thought twice about it, but now he wondered if the reports of ghosts were simply glitches.

The lack of ghosts seemed to get Ryan thinking about what

ifs. "Actually," he said, "there's Proverbs 30:14. 'There are those whose teeth are swords, whose fangs are knives, to devour the poor from off the earth, the needy from among mankind.' I don't think it directly meant blood drinking creatures. But there's also lines in Revelations that say, 'For they have shed the blood of saints and prophets, and you have given them blood to drink. It is what they deserve.' The only other thing I can remember is a line in Leviticus, but I think it's just similar to the rest of that book and demands you don't do things."

"Okay, so vampires are a no go, but what about true name lore?" Rebecca asked.

"Oh! Yeah, that's covered too." Ryan pulled a couple of flashlights out, turned them on, and set them up on a nearby chest of drawers. "There's Yahweh, which some people stopped using to avoid taking God's name in vain. Jehovah became a translated version of that later on. The divine name is actually a source of infighting between faiths, and even certain branches of Christianity itself."

Andrew frowned. "I thought Yahweh meant I am?"

"Very Descartes of him," Rebecca added.

"It's a bit more complex than that," Ryan continued. "We were taught it's more, 'I will be with you'. Just look at Christmas songs that talk about Emmanuel rather than Jesus. Emmanuel means God's with us."

"See what I mean! God's real divine name could be Greg," Rebecca turned towards a new sound, only to realize it was rain hitting the glass. "That's a point for me."

"You didn't prove your point at all!" Andrew complained. "Ref?"

"Gonna rule in her favor here. While I don't believe God is named Greg in the slightest, the point that we don't know his true name in the modern sense holds."

They walked into another room to set up a meter. It was the third and last one for the house.

"Fine," Andrew said, "but then I wager that supernatural vampires did not exist in the Bible."

"That's cheating," Ryan said. "And could we please focus on the possible paranormal currently around us?"

Ryan turned on an Ovilus device. It started up with disjointed sounds as it tried to convert environmental data into speech. The idea behind it was that if a spirit could create a cold spot, it would have an easier time talking through a device that read those inputs.

"If there's a ghost here," he said, "know we are here to help."

A light on the box lit up as the speaker played an electronic sound. "Yes."

"Are you stuck here?"

The box made another short sound, a beep, really, that could only be another one syllable word. Ryan moved around the room, and it made more noises, like a game of hot and cold. The "hottest" spot in the room was the closet. He glanced around the area overfilled with clothes, then he looked up and pointed out wood panels that led up to the attic. Here, the Ovilus really got working, but no one picked up what it was saying.

When Ryan stepped back, Andrew leaned in for a look himself. "Ghost or not, that could explain why they are hearing noises from the attic. That piece of ceiling isn't covered like the rest. Wait, I think it's an access point." He reached up and slid a board over. It was unclear if he could climb up further to access the whole attic, or just one very large pipe.

"That's weird," Rebecca declared, without seeing it for herself. She stopped to look at a series of photos arranged on a dresser. Two of the frames were face down, either from falling down or someone not wanting to see them. The rest were of the family, some of whom she had seen today. "Very cute Mom, though."

"You mentioned that already," Andrew laughed.

"It's worth re-mentioning!"

Ryan put down a couple of devices and readied another before gesturing to the door. "Come on, let's go check the kid's room."

The stuff inside didn't seem to quite fit the room. There was a rectangle window in the outside wall that threw everything off. If it hadn't been horizontal, everything would have looked as if it was designed to fit in here. Instead, the top corner of a bunk bed/desk combo blocked it. Everything was pushed against the wall, besides a fallen stuffed animal.

"Why are children's rooms so creepy?" Rebecca asked. She stood at the door. When Andrew raised an eyebrow, waiting for her to come in, she shrugged. "This is the smallest room of the house, and I'm new at this. I'll just get in the way."

Andrew shrugged and ducked behind the camera. "They're creepy because the presumption of innocence no matter what. It's why I hate churches."

Rebecca frowned and opened her mouth to reply when the sound of a knock rippled through the hallway. She jumped. "What was on this land before this?"

Her voice sounded shaky. Luckily, Ryan had the answer. "It was farmland."

"Cool, so if the dad was right and it's just a little ghost girl from a farm? That's not so bad, not too evil."

This time Andrew and Ryan shared a look, both asking the other not to say anything. It was commonly thought that demons often took the form of little girls. The presumption of innocence, Andrew thought to himself.

Rebecca shuddered. "'Stay in the house, Becca,'" she rambled, "'It will be better than the truck. It will be like a rental for the night.' I'd rather be squished."

"You still can stay in the truck," Andrew said.

"Don't tempt me, my guitar is out there."

Ryan brought their sleeping bags into the bedroom since that was where the homeowners reported the most activity. The plan had been for someone to stay in the kids' room, but that had died after the Ovilus kept going off.

There was such a thing as safety in numbers, but Andrew wondered if having near-homeless kids stay in haunted places was reckless endangerment or not. His worry ticked up to ten when he heard the creak of a door. A few minutes later, another creak planted a seed of hope as Rebecca came in. The beautifully natural sound of an acoustic guitar dispelled the rest of his fears and made morning come around quick.

The homeowners brought them a breakfast of coffee and donuts. Once again, life felt like a church event - people gathered together, sharing food and drink while a priest went around providing reassurance. "If we pick up anything else in the audio review," Ryan said, "I'll be sure to give you a call."

"Thank you all for coming out so fast," the very cute mother said. She looked back at the house as they all stood outside. "Everything feels a little brighter already."

CHAPTER TWELVE

As they traveled, assorted sleeping arrangements became a bigger and bigger annoyance. The lack of consistency caused as much trouble as anything else. Even Frank, the lamp, had been moved to several spots in the truck, failing to find its own space.

"How about this one?"

Rebecca stretched out her arm across the cab holding out her phone for Ryan in the driver's seat. Her back was to the door, and her hand only made it halfway over her outstretched legs. Parking had its benefits.

Ryan looked up from his own search to see a photo of a white van that had been converted into a mobile library. Two seats remained upfront, and solid wood crates were stacked along the inside walls. Outside was a table with even more wood crates and books out for display. It seemed like an adorable way to have a bookstore ready for a flea market circuit, but less viable as a home on wheels.

"Very cute," Ryan said, "but not all that helpful for our purposes."

"Yeah, I guess that's true." She slid down in her seat a little.

"I'm mostly worried about those conversions because they never retain more than two seats. Where will we all sit?"

"Aw, it's fine. Throw Andrew in the back." Rebecca sat up and knocked on the truck's back window. The noise caught Andrew's attention, who was actually already back there. She held up her hand, alternating between an otherwise neutral thumb up or down. He flashed a down and went back to his own research.

Rebecca looked back at the photo. "I can't figure out how they avoid books falling when they turn."

"What gets me is the bullshit of people listing cars at like a dollar for the clicks." Ryan sighed. "I mean, no one is going to sell a van with a clear title for six dollars."

"Six?"

"As in thousand, but they're cheating the search price options by just saying six."

"Rude."

"Amen to that."

Rebecca's phone chimed with a text. She read aloud from what Andrew sent. "'I thought I found the perfect one. Red, older, so not super expensive. THREE CUP HOLDERS.'"

"He thought?" Ryan asked, and had to wait for a follow up text that soon came.

"'The back is already cleared out but super creepy.'" Rebecca showed Ryan the attached photo of the back. Faux wood paneling started from the top and curved all the way around the sides and doors, only stopping at new pale blue carpeting.

"That's where murders happen," Ryan said.

Rebecca's phone chimed twice more in quick succession. Andrew must have heard him. "'Not with light colored carpet,'" Rebecca said. "He also says, 'OMG THATS WHY IT DOESN'T MATCH.'

"A no go then?" Ryan laughed.

"Not unless you want to exorcise a possible crime scene."

Ryan shrugged, and put his phone down. "Maybe we should just go to a used car lot and see what they got."

Summoned forward by the sound of the truck's engine starting, Andrew emerged from the back. Rebecca squeezed over to the middle to let him in.

There was a used car lot about twenty minutes away, and to their blessing, it was comprised of two different businesses that shared one very large lot full of cars. Guest parking wasn't clearly marked, so Ryan pulled into the first opening he saw. No one greeted them right away, even though it seemed like workers were walking around.

When they were greeted, it was by a stranger who encouraged the laissez faire selling tactic: "Do you until you're ready." They walked down an aisle of trucks and vans. Their options were exclusively white on white on white, with one huge exception. One van was decked out with green, blue, and orange scales. The wrap was designed to look like a large lizard ripped through to loom next to a red and yellow striped snake that wrapped around some pet shop's name. There was a URL below, but none of them bothered to look it up. They figured that if the van was here, the pet store must be done for.

"Wow, can you imagine if we rolled up in that?" Andrew asked, peeking through tinted windows that made it tricky to see inside.

"I cannot," Ryan confessed. "It's the right size at least."

"Hey, look at this one!" Rebecca called from behind them.

She was standing by a VW van - not the two-zoned classic with rounded edges, but a Crafter, white with black trim, and most importantly, large. She seemed to be counting as they walked over. "Seating for nine, and the headroom! Volkswagens are always great on that front."

The paperwork in the window listed it as a long plus wheelbase, which had to make it among the most spacious out there. It would need a lot of modifications to be a true camper, but it definitely was the sort of car that people converted into a custom RV. It also seemed wasteful to rip out perfectly good seats in a vehicle that was listed at ten thousand, but it was probably the most room they would get unless they converted a school bus.

"I'm going to go find the guy who greeted us," Ryan said, glancing to the kids. "See if we can test drive it."

He returned a short time later with the keys, and held them up with a little shake. Two heads popped up, likely distracted from looking for flaws they could use to haggle. "They are super chill here," he said. "I just had to let them photocopy my ID. I like it."

They hopped inside. Andrew let out a resounding *Ooooohhhh* that caught everyone's attention. "I thought vans with all windows like this were like, whited out, and no one could see in or out. Not that some were a privacy screen. That makes it far less dark and creepy."

Rebecca ignored his dismay, vaguely gesturing as if her movements were as good as a measuring tape. "I think we could do two covered benches, you know, the type with storage under. And then one along the end makes a U shape that gives us enough sleeping room without giving up all of the floor space."

Andrew swung an arm around her shoulders. "Rebecca Grace, you're a true visionary."

"Buckle up," Ryan said. "First, we gotta test if it runs, and if the chairs are comfortable enough to get us by for a few." Ryan started the engine and waited until they were both buckled up before pulling onto the road. He didn't go far, just up the street and over to a wide side road where he could break the speed limit to make sure it would survive highway speeds. There were no stray sounds or odd shaking while idling at a stop sign. It had a number of miles on but not more than what he would expect for its year. After the test drive, that just left the haggling.

Despite the size of the lot, most of that was taken up by cars and an onsite mechanic. A small, narrow one-room building with two desks stacked one behind the other was where business was done. Andrew and Rebecca stepped in, but the small size made it easier to just waited outside.

Andrew crossed his arms, then just as quickly uncrossed them. To kill time, Rebecca walked over to a pair of white Beetles. They were an older style than the one she had, but she still ran her hand over them like she wanted them.

By the time she noticed him again, Andrew was practically radiating anxiety. "What are you freaking out about?"

He licked his lips, glancing towards the door. "Ryan isn't rich. I don't know how much money he has, but I know it isn't a lot to throw around. I'm honestly surprised we are even looking at a van this nice. I thought we'd have to trade the truck for a grungy van and use whatever was left to try to work something out."

"Oh," Rebecca said. "I guess I never really thought about that."

Andrew scoffed, shaking his head. For the first time, he was truly annoyed with her. It was nearing two months since they'd met online, and as much as he wanted to help her escape a life she didn't like, he also was surprised she was still with slumming it with them.

"I'm sorry," she said, like she'd heard his thoughts. "I know I come off like a privileged asshole sometimes, and I know I didn't find my first truck stop shower experience as liberating as you, but I've gotten to play in parks as the sun rises. I can finally change the pronouns in songs for the first time without fear, and go on weird adventures with people who let be me. This might not be as glitzy as my old life, but it's everything."

"Whatever," he said, trying to deflect. He knew that yelling "you better not bail" at her wasn't fair either. Ryan hadn't demanded a commitment to stay when he first joined. "As long as you help make this new space awesome, it's all good."

"I promise, it's going to be awesome."

Buying a vehicle took longer than Ryan had told them it

would. There was haggling, and then calling a manager to get the approval, then going to the bank to get cash and the paperwork for trading the truck in to help pay for it all. And then, on top of everything, they had to drive to another building to actually sign that paperwork. Despite how many workers they had spotted walking around, the finance department was just one person who was already making a sale.

When all was said and done, the boys were standing outside a fast food place and waiting for Rebecca to use the bathroom. Both vehicles sat in the parking lot. It felt strange to think they wouldn't be returning to the truck.

"You okay?"

Ryan seemed confused as he looked over, as if the words didn't register at first. He smiled, even if Andrew wasn't sure if he should believe it. "Of course."

"This is going to sound random, but did you ever want to be a father?"

Ryan laughed nervously. "Uh, that wasn't ever in the plan."

Andrew nodded as if he understood. "You'd make a good one."

"Sorry I took so long," Rebecca said, coming from a direction they hadn't expected. "I wanted to pick up something. It's a gift to open up in the van." She held up a plastic bag with the straps tied up for Ryan.

They all piled into the van, Ryan in the front and Rebecca and Andrew in the second row. They watched as he undid the easy plastic knot. Inside was a wrist lanyard made up of translucent blue beds with a lobster clip hanging off. "Aw," Ryan said, "for my new keys."

Rebecca smiled. "I noticed you kept the Ray charm from your old set, but you didn't put it on the new set. So, I thought you could loop this around the rear-view mirror and display it that way."

Ryan quickly dug into his pocket to give it a try. A small ray shined through, making the van instantly more personal.

"It's great, thank you."

When night came, Andrew moved back a row of seats, sitting in one and putting his legs up across another as a makeshift bed. Behind him was all their gear. Even to Ryan, who sat on his phone with his arms crossed over the wheel, there felt like a good amount of room.

Rebecca moved up to the passenger seat next to him, in part for the light from the console so she could read.

"Hey, do you still have that Spanish Palms decal?" Ryan asked.

"Yeah?"

He gestured to the windshield. "Did you want to put it in the window?"

"It's silly. I don't know why I even keep it."

"Yes, you do," he said, smiling.

Rebecca looked at him for a long moment before pulling it out of her bag. Gingerly, she smoothed it out flat over her lap. "It's the last place I really felt at home. We moved to California a few years ago, for the band. I didn't want to, so I kept it. Like I could refuse to admit that we moved. I guess my new home is a good spot for it."

Ryan briefly frowned. "You don't have to stay with us."

Rebecca glanced back to check if Andrew was asleep. "I know. But I've been thinking about a shelf for that silly cat lamp, so I don't think they're real when I see them from the corner of my eye. Hell, if I get really creative, I might be able to outfit multiple bunk beds so you can pick up even more kids."

"Please don't," Ryan laughed.

"I won't," she said. She was laughing now too. "If I'm honest, I'm making dreams up as I go. Yesterday, I absolutely wanted to find two more girls and start a three sisters' band. Decided our stage names would be themed after a trio of mountains. As if that was the ultimate end game goal."

"That's a good one."

"Yeah, but I guess until I find two more lesbian musicians, I'm content with making this van more charming." She leaned forward, and stuck that important square of plastic in the bottom of the window.

CHAPTER THIRTEEN

The rain sounded different in the van. With the camper, they'd open a window to get not only the smell of rain, but the sound of it, as if you were standing outside. The van made it feel more distant, like there could be a record downpour and you'd be just as snug as you were on a day without a single cloud.

Rebecca listened to the rain's light sound as it bounced off the roof, still half asleep. Once she knew she was going to stay awake she turned, cuddling up against the back of the futon sofa sleeper they'd picked up, and watched the rain run off the windows. The sleeper sofas didn't have wooden storage underneath like they originally planned, but sometimes changed plans worked out better. Her guitar wouldn't have fit otherwise, and the bed's feet even kept it from sliding around when they were on the move.

Andrew originally hadn't been too convinced they had needed a trip to IKEA, but he got into it more after walking around all the tiny living examples. Now, tucked above his feet and behind the passenger seat was a small drop leaf table. Frank lived on the middle piece, but they still sometimes got moved around, specifically towards the back for puzzle night.

It took time to pull the seats out without destroying the car, or their own fingers in the process. In the end, it wasn't a very high-end conversation, but it was functional for what they needed. And while minimalist wasn't Rebecca's favorite style, she started to see its merits.

Ryan was up first, as he usually was. He walked to the front to check his phone. Because the van conversion took some time, they had a small backlog of requests. In-between putting furniture together, Ryan set up a schedule. The next month and a half was tightly packed with cross country investigations, pit stops, and general travel.

Rebecca sat up, rubbing her eyes. The movement caught Ryan's attention. He quietly asked, "Ready to head somewhere for breakfast?"

"Just about. Andrew isn't awake yet, though."

"No worries," Ryan said, "he's like a cat. You're allowed to interrupt sleep as long as it means food."

Andrew was still yawning as they walked into a restaurant that named itself after the breakfast food it mainly served. When it came to non-chains, food was always either a home run or a strikeout. From the outside, it looked like the latter. At some point, it had been converted from something that once had a drive thru, which was now nothing more than a sunny counter for plants.

Inside, however, was completely updated. The short wall along the street was painted black and had alternating fonts and sizes making up a larger than life copy of the menu. Mostly, it comprised of pancakes and the various wild favors you could try, like red velvet and mint.

The other side was a feature wall, and what a feature it was. Short bits of wood ranging in both length and width were painted in soft yellows and darker purples, along with greens, oranges, greys, and pinks placed both directions.

"Wow, this looks as gay as I am," Andrew said, awake enough to finally hold a conversation. Only a few of the colors would have been found on the classic rainbow flag, but sections that had three stripes here, five there, certainly gave off that impression.

"Oh my god," Rebecca said, holding the menu up with two hands. "The Hangover Cure. Two half pound burgers topped with bacon, cheese, and egg between two buttermilk pancakes. That sounds disgusting. I can't imagine anyone hungover could actually eat that without losing their stomach."

"It works," Andrew said. Rebecca stared at him as if he was mumbling half asleep nonsense. "Greasy foods after a night of drinking."

She continued to stare in disbelief until she glanced back at her own menu.

Ryan leaned across the table towards Rebecca. "If it helps, I also think it's an old wives' tale."

"Have either of you been drunk? I'm telling you; it works." Andrew pulled out his phone and started to Google, but before the search engine won his point, a waitress came over to take their order. Andrew's order was mostly gesturing to the menu as if he couldn't pronounce the options. "With scrambled eggs please." The waitress nodded, making no mention of the fact that it was the only thing labeled for kids, and left to bring them water.

A different waiter dropped off their drinks. His ears were gauged, and he held himself like he was actually the owner of the place. He was young, definitely younger than Ryan, but older than Andrew, who was doing his best not to stare.

"Cute," Rebecca said leaning in, not wanting to be overheard. "Right?"

Andrew stared. "Shut up."

Rebecca celebrated her rightness with a fist pump.

It would have been nice to leave California and not come back. Especially once Rebecca's parents contacted her, asking her to come back. When she said no, they started trying to tell her how far she strayed from God's path. Maybe it was because she was traveling with a former pastor who could have likely joined their own church if he had asked, but to Rebecca, their threats didn't have as much punch as they would have. Before, just a look could have made her fall in line, but she said that even a taste of freedom was liberating.

Although, to be fair, with how big California was they were also seven hours away from that unholy mess. What did skirt the line was Andrew's willingness to investigate a former Catholic mission. Ryan tried to explain the differences between a mission and a church during the drive, but Rebecca summarized any of the technical points with: "So, like a tiny church?"

It was dark by the time they arrived, but things were left open, waiting for them. The building was old enough that everything had a heavy groan when moved.

Ghosts of clergy members were always rumored to be demonic in nature, especially if not fondly remembered. And this mission in particular had even more of a questionable start. When it came to misusing faith, the priest who once worked at this mission, Padre Jose Altimira, had to be among the more racist of them.

"Hola, mi nombre es Andrew," Andrew said, trying to remember everything he could from his year of Spanish. "Do you think they'd speak Spanish in the afterlife, or is it more of a universal translator sort of thing?"

"That would depend on what type of ghost you believed was here," Ryan said.

Rebecca took a look around, holding out a camera to capture whatever she was seeing. "And what type do you think it is?"

"Possible demon priest. You two are bonus eyes and ears."

"Mmm gross," Andrew said, shaking his head as he sat up a stationary camera. "Could you not list body parts." When he stopped speaking, he heard a hissing sound. He stood up straight staring at the others to silently ask if they heard that too.

"Finish up setting up," Ryan suggested. "I'm going to see what I can feel out. The alarms should be off for tonight, but if we venture too far you might trigger something."

"We'll be good church kids," Rebecca said, the joke clear in her silly grin.

Ryan smiled back. "Exactly what I'm worried about."

They didn't have the equipment of a bigger crew, so they walked the church grounds first to scope out the best vantage points for their stationary camera. Their roaming flashlights searched the halls.

"This Jesus statue looks like Benedict Cumberbatch."

Andrew stopped next to Rebecca and shined his own light on the statue. It was a classic Jesus pose: he stood with flowing robes; hands marked from being hung from the cross. One was out and low, the other pointed to a heart with thorns and a cross on top. His hair was long, flowing to one side, and by damn, that face did look like Benedict Cumberbatch.

"Shit, you're right. It's so weird. I can't stop looking at it." Dust floated in the air, falling slow enough that it was like time itself slowed. "Do you think Jesus would like always being shown with stigmata? I don't think I'd like my whole life to be defined by the most painful part of it."

"Wait, go back. Stig-whata?" Rebecca's thermal camera kept picking up a cold spot. It was probably just a window. She tried for a third time to angle her camera just right, to avoid the reflection.

"Stigmata. It's the crucifixion wounds in his hands."

"Oh, well, I can't imagine he cares. It's his whole deal." She gave the view screen a funny look before apparently deciding that she did her best. "I guess without them you wouldn't be able to tell it's the post-risen version of him."

"I asked Ryan once, and he said he liked seeing them. Said it made him feel closer to God. Showed that holiness didn't mean moving through the world without scars."

"That's poetic," Rebecca snorted. "I felt close to God when on stage, but it didn't protect me from homophobia."

Andrew opened his mouth to say that was the point, but decided against it. They walked back through the camera's frame, passing by the room with the statue again. Andrew stopped. He could barely see it. If it hadn't been made from white stone, he probably would have seen nothing at all.

"Andrew, you coming?" Rebecca called. "I can't do a proper spirit box session without your hand camera."

"Yeah, sorry. I'll be right there."

They moved into a long hall with photos framed and matted on each side. Rebecca picked a table at random to sit at, and placed the spirit box in the middle. Her hands cupped around it briefly, muffling the static. "Gah, do you ever get used to this sound?"

"Not really," Andrew said as he swung a leg over to sit down across from her. "That's why I almost like when it says words. Uh, I'm trying to think of what 'anyone' is in Spanish." It took a moment, but then he asked the air if anyone was there.

The sound skipped, like some signal was trying to cut through the static. "Come again?" Rebecca asked, and Andrew repeated it in Spanish in case it mattered. They waited, but Rebecca turned the box off before they heard anything clearly.

"Do you believe in ghosts or demons?" Andrew asked Rebecca.

"I don't know," she said. "I don't even really know if I'm Christian anymore. It was a title more given to me than anything else. Like my hair color."

"De-christian," he teased.

"Heretic."

"Sain't."

Rebecca tried to hold back her amusement, but when Andrew started grinning, they threw off the whole spooky vibe of the place by laughing. They had to let all of ridiculousness out before they were able to compose themselves. It was meant to be a professional and serious search. When they stopped and just waited for a moment, the place really did feel timeless, like they were sharing the same sights and sounds as people a hundred years ago did.

Rebecca panned the camera around, musing aloud. "You know, it is really weird that you could make a statue of like, any dude, and say it's him. As long as it isn't painted, everyone will usually accept it. Seems wrong. Is there not a description of what Jesus looked like?"

Andrew shrugged. "Guess not."

"False."

The voice echoed down the hall as a shadow followed along with it. Fear built, then vanished just like the silence before it when Ryan stepped into view.

"Luke says Jesus became wiser and taller, but not so tall he couldn't fit in among the people when he visits a temple."

"Point Ryan. Weird point, but winner."

"I take it you saw the statue?" Ryan asked, looking from one to the other. Their affirmations came in like mismatched notes of agreement. "It looks like Cesare Borgia with a blowout."

Rebecca laughed. Andrew asked, "Who?"

"Son of a Pope. Big crime family." When nothing clicked, Ryan added. "They made a TV show about the father being elected by the conclave, even included the part about his daughter acting in his place for a day?"

"Wow. I clearly don't know history, like at all." Andrew shook his head as another thought popped in. Perhaps that was why the thorns and wounds of Jesus mattered so much. They might be the only Christian symbolism that stayed true over time. His face didn't really matter, unless someone wanted to be racist and stubborn over their whitewashed version of him.

Rebecca, however, took the more non-denominational approach. "Catholicism is weird."

"Anyways," Andrew said, with an annoyed glance. He didn't believe, but Ryan did, and in a roundabout way that counted to him just as much. "How was your stakeout? Did you find anything. We... did not."

"Yeah, actually. That's why I came back to way to find you. Follow me."

Ryan led them to the chapel proper, down a path they had not ventured themselves. Two dots of light gleamed like eyes through open doors. Judging by the sound of their footsteps, this room was good for sound. It made the whole space stretch out beyond its dimensions. Once they finished slowly creeping up to the front of the room, Andrew saw that those eyes turned out to be small flashlights left out on the altar.

Andrew glanced around, trying to see anything of note. Being wide eyed was standard here. When no ghost was triggered like a switch from a haunted house, both kids looked towards Ryan, whose attention was solely on Rebecca.

"You should sing something."

"What?"

"Sing."

The air grew cold. None of the trio moved. The hairs on Rebecca's arms rose, like something had to be standing behind her.

"I... What song do you want?"

"You pick."

She glanced over to Andrew, who was now also watching her. He tried to give her an encouraging smile, but it came out weak. He didn't have an idea of what the plan was either.

Looking scared, like she was not sure she could remember the notes to anything, she picked something she told Andrew she'd memorized from childhood. Where most kids had learned things like The Wheels on the Bus, she'd been taught a much harder song from the book of Exodus.

She exhaled shakily. As the temperature dropped, she started to sing the Song of Miriam.

The words didn't matter. After the first verse, it was hard to even pick them out as her voice echoed back at different times. The room was alive, like there were three of them all singing a round of the same hymn. As Rebecca realized why she was brought here, growing triumph could be heard in each voice.

Ryan grinned. "I found your three sisters."

The footsteps and voices that had terrified so many who entered this house of God, one that had been stained in hate and outright war, was now replaced by an unending chorus full of surprise, wonder, and joy. Rebecca's song choice really hadn't mattered, back then, or now. *She* was as angelic a creature as any.

CHAPTER FOURTEEN

"This post theorizes that maybe only cats become ghosts, since it would explain why the most reported activity tends to be bumps in the night or things being knocked off tables."

Andrew looked up at Rebecca. It was an odd day already, given that the van was in the shop for an oil change that turned into an overnight tune up, so he gave the comment a moment's thought. Only one, however. "The Internet is rotting your brain. This is why you should watch more cartoons." There was no real ill will there, simply the desire to convert more people to the holy ritual of Saturday morning cartoon days. Those were as rare as miracles.

Rebecca gestured to the thick boxy television mounted between the two windows of their rectangle-shaped hotel room. "It's just hard to focus when my heart can't get over what they did to Sonic Boom."

"...What did they do to Sonic Boom?"

"If you don't know, I don't have the heart to tell you."

Andrew stared at her as if she was being deadly serious, before realizing she wasn't. Then he picked up a pillow and hurled it at her.

"It's for your own protection," she mocked cried. She picked up the thrown pillow and hugged it. The phone she'd been reading off of now sitting upside down on the bed. "I actually think I have my parents' log-in, if you want to watch some more."

"Rebecca... You've been holding out on me this whole time?"

"Oh, hush. We'll need a cord to we can hook it up to the TV, so we don't have to hover over my phone."

"God bless technology. Tell me what cord you need and consider it done."

Rebecca got up, leaning her head near the TV so she could see in the tight gap between the wall. "HDMI will do it."

"On it," Andrew declared. He got up and headed out to find the fabled cord that would create a cartoon-filled morning.

The elevator dinged as it opened. Andrew took his first steps down the stairs, and Ryan called after him. "Hey, hold up. Where are you going?"

"I gotta get something from the gas station, is the car done?"

"Needs a few more hours."

"Well, I'll be back before then."

"I'd hope so."

Andrew laughed to himself and took another step down before Ryan stopped him again.

"Hey! Um, I need to talk to you about something."

"Can it be after?"

"Yeah, sure." Ryan ran a hand through his hair, nodding in agreement. "Grab everyone breakfast while you're out, okay?"

Andrew pulled out his wallet to see how much cash he had on him. Definitely enough for a gas station shopping spree.

"Sure thing, boss."

The chain on the corner of their hotel was actually Andrew's favorite for its killer coffee, and some made the best breakfast burritos of his life. He hoped he could find some and bring a trio back to share with Rebecca and Ryan. Wandering around the store, he found the needed cord, coffee for himself, donuts because breakfast burritos were a strike out, and a thought he hadn't really given too much attention until now.

Andrew stared at the milk cartons, wondering if he had ever seen a missing photo on the side of one. *When had that stopped being a thing? Had plastic ruined missing kid searches?* He shook the thought off, checked out, and headed back to the hotel.

Without ad breaks, cartoons went by quick. Within an hour, they had watched the first five episodes. By the end, one consensus was reached, by Andrew, at least.

"You're the Tails," he said. Rebecca tossed a hand in the air as a silent objection as he went on, "The sidekick."

Her outrage melted as she thought of a new idea. "Actually, I can live with that. Instead of *being* Amy, does that mean I get to *date* her?"

"I— uh." Andrew looked to Ryan for help of some sort, but they didn't share a glance long enough to get Andrew any sort of reply. "This is taking us down a fandom path I am not ready for and I take it all back."

"Knuckles is my favorite," Ryan declared. They knew he had been watching, but Andrew didn't realize he'd been paying attention. "There's just something about him that I like."

"He'd a good dude. Good…porcupine?" Rebecca picked up her phone to fact check herself. "I don't even know how to say that, so let's stick with dude."

Ryan's phone rang. The screen showed the mechanic's number, so instead of excusing himself like before, he took the call. The interaction lasted less than a minute, and then he declared to the rest of the room that their van was ready. They packed up, and hung around for the courtesy shuttle to pick them up. The waiting turned into more waiting, since other people were also standing around hoping to get their car back soon. As they sat in a little corner of the shop by a vending machine, Ryan's phone went off for the third time that day.

"Hey man, it's me."

Andrew could overhear the call even if it hadn't been put on speaker, curiosity growing as Ryan's expression seemed one of recognition as he spoke.

"Patrick? It's been a while, what's up?"

"I heard you're hunting ghosts now; thought I could lure you in to investigate something for me."

"Sounds ominous, but you aren't wrong. What's going on?"

"I'd rather tell you the details in person, but uh, I'm pretty sure I might be haunted. Stuff has moving around in my apartment and I thought maybe it was just poor memory. I've come out to visit some people in Utah, and it's *still* happening."

"We can definitely check it out for you. We are a ways out, though, so it will be a few days."

"That's fine, I'll send you the address of where I'm staying."

Rebecca stepped forward, holding the newly re-acquired keys up to silently signal they were ready.

"Sounds good," Ryan said. "I'll talk to you more soon."

Andrew had thought about asking more about the call, but a debate had broken out by the time they made it to the van. He was emphatic that he had left Yoshi on his bed. Rebecca shrugged her shoulders.

"Maybe it's possessed."

Andrew picked Yoshi up off the passenger seat. "Yoshi, are you stuffed with fluff and ghosts?" He waited a beat. "Naw, Yoshi would tell me."

CHAPTER FIFTEEN

"I have gathered you together to declare I have officially become nocturnal," Rebecca said, her eyes on the road. There wasn't much to be seen between the two headlines shining in an otherwise pitch-black night.

Andrew glanced over from the passenger seat. He was tired, but Ryan was already sleeping in the back, and Andrew was determined to keep her company. It was working, just not comfortably.

"Really, it's fine. Go to bed."

Andrew sat up, as if his posture would convince her that he wasn't that tired after all. "You won't let me drive, so I'm supervising."

"That's not-" Rebecca laughed softly. "You're a pretty relaxed super, my hands aren't even at ten and two."

Andrew glanced at the wheel, narrowing his eyes. Sure enough, they weren't. She wasn't driving poorly. It was just something you'd lose a point for if it had been a driving test. "As long as you can drive straight, that's all the matters."

"It's about the only thing I *can* do straight."

"You win." He smiled before he got up. "Just promise to wake me so I can do my share, please."

When morning came, the shift had changed. They drove out of one town that started with an M, and entered another that might have had an I, if memory served the boys correctly. Normally, one of their collective phones had enough signal to pull up a map, but it was a signal dead zone and the human brain was a forgetful thing.

Ryan pulled the van off to the side of the road. "Can you take over? I'm going to try to restart my phone, see if I can get a text to Patrick through." Glancing over his shoulder, Ryan saw that Rebecca was awake, but she was pretending to still be asleep because she didn't want to get up.

As if sensing a growing tension, Rebecca sat up, feet barely on the floorboard. She eyed Ryan as he headed to the back before taking herself up to the passenger seat. "Where are we?" she asked, mid-yawn.

"Utah."

Rebecca shook her head, smiling. "Well, I'd hope so by now."

Meeting at a hotel in Utah was to be expected. However, meeting at the hotel bar went against everything Ryan thought he knew about the state's distaste for alcohol. The initial awkwardness of not seeing someone for years quickly dissolved, as if it were the old days in college when they knew they were all on their own, and therefore weren't. There didn't even seem like they had much to "catch up on," so Ryan seamlessly got down to the business at hand.

"What spirit did you want me to investigate?"

Patrick slid his rum over in front of Ryan before signaling to the bartender. Ryan's eyes stayed on the woman as she had to go through the extra steps of obscuring where it was being poured from before she brought the drink. *Utah,* he thought to himself.

The ease Ryan felt before vanished. "Are you kidding me?"

Patrick downed the new drink. When Ryan didn't seem interested in the first, he pulled it back to his side. "Not really. I thought you discussed spirits."

Ryan huffed, shaking his head to an audience of none. "Yeah, the *paranormal* type."

Patrick put down his glass, turning to get a real look at Ryan again. "You really believe in that stuff? I thought you went the life coach route since you quit being a priest."

"What gave you that idea?"

"When I got off the phone with Father Michael…" Patrick started to explain, but Ryan looked at him as if he wasn't saying real words. "Isn't that what all priests do anyways? Except their paranormal being is God."

"Jesu—"

"Ah!" Patrick held up a finger and Ryan let the word trail off. "See, exactly." He sounded pleased with himself, even though he didn't really make a point at all.

The theatrics of it all made Ryan crack a smile at least.

"Give it back." Ryan gestured to the glass.

With a brow raised, Patrick watched his friend finish it off, stifling a laugh as Ryan's face went askew. "You used to handle that better."

Ryan pressed a hand to his mouth, letting out a muffled comment about how he was getting old and that drinking was always awful. "I should go," he said, clearing his throat. "I have kids in the car."

"Kids? What the- we clearly failed at catch up. Just stay, talk. I'll give you whatever your going rate is."

"If you don't drink all your money away."

Patrick leaned back in his seat, pulling a stack of bills out and dropping them on the counter. "One rule: No more rudeness. If you won't liberate these spirits from their glasses,

I want nostalgia tonight." He paused. "They aren't, like, tiny, are they?"

"One is seventeen, the other is nineteen."

Patrick blinked, mentally doing the math and coming up with more questions than he had before. In the end he waved a hand at it all. "See, practically adults. You came all this way, get your pay, man."

Ryan thought about it. The great and terrible thing about his friend was that he was always the most interesting person in the room. That terrified Ryan when he was closeted, but then Patrick got kicked out, and after that, Ryan stopped hiding himself away in the first place. "Okay, for old times' sake."

"Fuck the past," Patrick claimed, sending a mixed message that Ryan doubted would get any clearer from here on. "Tell me about you now."

Patrick continued to drink, stealing Ryan's share without any complaints as they shared the past few years. Ryan sat there, snacking on pub mix and thinking to himself more than listening when Patrick started to amuse himself by describing things as "spirits of his past" and his exploits with women he met on the road. Then Ryan thought about how low someone must be to call a paranormal investigator just for a chat. It dawned on him how similar "how low" could sound like "hallow." Their connection to each other both tragic and divine.

Drinking always has a deterioration, a self-destruction to it, and he'd seen Patrick's slide into being wasted enough realize times to know that the process was always a slow creep, one that people rarely saw until they were away from that cliff and looking back at what they narrowly avoided. Like depression.

"Suicide by ghost," Ryan mumbled, in the middle of Patrick's story.

"What?"

"Sorry, your story made me realize something." Ryan wondered what would have happened if Patrick had called to reminisce before he met Andrew and accidentally started a found family. Before he found hope in new people. "We've both been a bit lost. Chasing spirits, if you will."

Patrick nodded.

Ryan only barely felt like he was making sense, but the encouragement allowed him to continue. "Before, I left out the part where I had been taunting ghosts. Wanting them to do something, pushing my luck. That was before I found people to care about *because* of this new life. Family is what matters. And I'm not talking about the people that *should* have been there, I mean the people you find who *are.*"

Patrick snorted. "You realized all of that because of something I said? Ha, maybe I should be a life coach."

"You and me? We are still family," Ryan declared. "Do you need help?"

"Yeah," Patrick said. He had sobered, but only in tone.

"Tell me what I can do for you."

"Man, I think it would be great if there were ghosts. Like, just picture it." Patrick gestured with one arm out in front of him, almost bumping his hand into Ryan's chest. He was being carried toward his room, too drunk otherwise without Ryan's support. "Suddenly, all of this bullshit wouldn't matter. Maybe there'll be a monster under the bed with something to prove it! Pfft, no monster is going to blow its cover that way. It would need to have a serious foot fetish to even dare."

Ryan cringed, largely at Patrick's varying volume rather than the topic of monsters having kinks. Not that it was a topic he had much interest in, either. "That certainly would be telling."

"How would they even get there? The under the bed type isn't a wild animal. Makes no sense."

Thankfully the hotel only had one floor, leaving Ryan with the final step of trying to pull the key card out of his pocket with one hand so he didn't have to prop his friend up. "Maybe it's like *Monsters, Inc.*?"

"What?"

"You know, with the portals being the closet door." The lock on the door in front of them flashed green, and Ryan maneuvered them inside.

"Huh. Wait a minute, didn't that movie end with stand-up comedy protecting kids?"

"Uh," Ryan stalled. He'd wanted to carefully help his friend to the bed, but with the weight shifting, he more... spilled Patrick onto the bed, just barely able to free his own arm in time. "That's one way to look at it."

"I remember." Patrick tapped on the side of his head. "Steel trap."

Ryan placed the keycard on the TV stand, swapping it for car keys in case Patrick decided he needed to drive himself through a vending machine in the middle of the night. "I'll meet up with you in the morning to give these back. Call me when you wake up."

Patrick yawned like Ryan wasn't even in the room and rolled over on his side, feet curled up.

Ryan walked back to the van, and nearly had a heartache when he saw it was empty.

"Ryan said to stay here," Rebecca said, guitar in her lap. "I'm out of practice, but am I so bad you have to flee the sound?"

"Ryan also said we were ghost hunting." Andrew leaned out of the driver's door. "Come on, consider it recon."

Their scouting mission consisted of walking down the street looking for anything that jumped out at them, both literally and figuratively. The paved portion of the road ended abruptly, turning into a side dirt path. Traffic signs reflected back under flashlights, and a lighted board read BEWARE with a series of characters that looked alien before finishing with a misspelled version of "ahead" in caps on the last line.

"The Scooby-Doo gang would check that out," Andrew said.

"We gotta, then."

This path didn't have much besides large trees and bushes along one side away from the street, and whatever else was "HAEAD." Since this area lacked many buildings, someone had painted graffiti down below in the dirt.

Maybe it should have concerned them, or hinted that they were in a bad area, but in truth it just reminded Andrew of kids with sidewalk chalk or finger paints on a wall. They were all placing color where their parents didn't want it.

"Hey," Andrew whispered to Rebecca.

"Yeah?" she whispered back.

"Do you think any ghosts are gay?"

That surprised her enough that she stopped walking. "Huh?"

"I don't mean if it's statically likely. Just like, I never really thought about it before. What if the unfinished business was that the ghost never came out?"

"The number of years we hid it was hard enough, I can't imagine being like, two hundred and still keeping that secret."

It was late. Andrew inhaled before yelling into the darkness: "Hey, we gay!"

Rebecca laughed. "Did you just come out to the ghosts?"

"Maybe." Andrew shrugged. "It's fun."

Rebecca didn't look so sure. She glanced at him, then looked up ahead, even behind, as if someone else living or dead was out here with them. She chewed on her lip before making up her mind. "I like girls!" she yelled.

As if someone did hear them, Rebecca's phone rang. The screen lit up with a photo of Ryan driving, taken from her spot in the van. She answered, "Oh hey, what's up?"

Andrew barely heard Ryan's question: "Where are you?"

"Down the street a bit, ghost hunting in your honor, or so

Andrew convinced me." She paused to listen. "Yeah sure, we'll be right there. See you soon."

"Back home we go?" Andrew asked as she hung up.

"Back home we go."

"Are you going to go?"

Ryan knew it was a loaded question, even though he wished he could ask without it being so. Everything always looked different in the morning. It was easy to ask for help in the moment, and much harder when daylight made things easier to ignore.

"We'll see," Patrick said. "I mean your mom doesn't like me. I doubt she wants to do me any favors."

"It's not a favor, it's part of her job. She didn't like you because you kept bringing girls to our dorm room and she thought someone was going to out me."

Patrick paused, trying to recall that.

"Steel trap, eh?" Ryan teased.

"I remember the number you gave me, and that's what's important."

"Mhm, be sure to call it. Or I'm going to get bonus calls from her about the lack of yours."

"Ah, family."

They hugged, the one arm over each other sort, before Patrick gave a quick wave to the teens who were waiting outside the van.

They stayed there until Patrick headed back into his room. "Do you think he's going to go?" Rebecca asked.

Ryan shrugged. "He has the information, sometimes that's all you can do."

"Speaking of phone calls, if you ever got tired of traveling," Andrew said in a tone that made him sound like a salesman. "I found an article that mentioned some exorcists are now doing their work by phone."

"That surely can't be allowed."

"Just listen." Andrew pulled out his phone, reading from an article that he'd already prepared. "'I do four or five a day with my phone'. I think it's an Italian priest, but still. That should make it more legit since it's closer to Rome, right?"

While Ryan stumbled over vowels, Rebecca snickered to herself. "You looking to settle down somewhere?"

"I was thinking maybe we could drive around to scenic locations, instead of..." Andrew gestured to the parking lot. "Oh! Italy makes sense now."

Ryan smiled. "You looking to go to Italy?"

"I'd need my parents' help to get a passport if we went now, so that's out."

At that comment, Ryan made a face. "About that. Father Michael called when we were waiting for the van, and he mentioned them."

"Fuck them."

"Andrew, please. We should talk about this." Ryan glanced at Rebecca. She took a step towards the van to give them room.

"You can stay," Andrew said quickly, glancing back for a second before meeting Ryan's eye. "The point of coming here was family, right? Spill it."

Ryan scratched at his face, unsure. Pressing seemed like it would be worse. "Okay. They uh, are claiming they sent you to a boarding school that streamlines students into a private college."

"So, no missing person report? No 'our son is missing,' at all?" Andrew asked. Ryan shook his head. "Good. Fuck them. If they can't avoid losing face, at least I'm free."

"You really okay with this?"

"Yeah." Andrew shook his head a little, looking more confused about why this was a big deal than stressed out by the news. "A couple more months and we'll really be home free. We can go anywhere without worry."

Rebecca stepped up next to Andrew, playfully bumping into him. "Maybe Italy."

"Pope's too powerful for me," Ryan teased. "Man got rid

of a circle of hell. Just wiped a whole plane of existence out of being."

"What?" Andrew said, growing more serious than he had at any other point. WiFi quickly allowed for on-the-fly fact checking. "'Purgatory was an unduly restrictive view of salvation.' Huh, well, shit. That *is* powerful."

"What are they going to say next?" Rebecca asked, leaning in to read off his phone. "That the afterlife isn't something you have to die for? That it's just your life after the bad? Wait, are purgatory and limbo the same thing?"

"They are not," Ryan clarified, "but who's to say your theology is wrong? It's just as hopeful and redemptive as any."

Andrew moved to sit in the driver's seat, shaking the keys like a game show prize. "Where does the Book of Ryan say we are going next?"

"The afterlife." Ryan nodded to himself. "Somewhere where we are needed, somewhere scenic."

The van's dome light provided a halo-like glow over Andrew's head. Ryan and Rebecca joined in, and then they all glowed as the sun rose.

Acknowledgments

Even solo adventures are aided by others, so a thanks goes out to Kristyn Knott and John Lopez. Their love and work on this novella strengthened this road trip.

About The Author

Rose Sinclair is still waiting for their Starfleet uniform to arrive, but isn't so picky about color. Until then they spend their time writing about magic, the morally grey, and articles that would warrant the title of cyberpunk beatnik. Any extra time would ideally be spent looking for plot bunnies, but in reality, likely used blogging about LGBTQ issues.

Also Check Out

Bone Diggers by Alexandra Tauber & Rose Sinclair

When everyone IRL lies, the only person you can trust is an NPC. Dirty little secrets can't be hidden behind player avatars, because Bone Diggers like Owen expose the lives behind the code. When Owen's two worlds blur, he must decide which is more important: his freedom, or the game. The right choices will be rewarded with fame, fortune, and adventure. A wrong call can cost him both lives. But playing the game is what Owen does, and he's good at it... as long as his real-life adventures don't prove more perilous than his digital swordfights. In the real world, there is no walkthrough.

Printed in Poland
by Amazon Fulfillment
Poland Sp. z o.o., Wrocław

50733475R00070